MERMAID OF VENICE

BOOK ONE

JINCEY LUMPKIN

To request permissions, contact the publisher at jincey@jinceylumpkin.com

Ebook: 978-1-7364712-0-3
Print: 978-1-7364712-2-7

CIP Block/Library of Congress Number: TXu002226850

First E-Book edition January 2021.

Edited by Amanda E. Clark
Cover art by Jason Brooks
Cover art direction by Matthew Axe
Cover layout by Lauren Balistreri

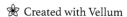 Created with Vellum

This book is dedicated to my brilliant and beautiful mother, Gail, who always believed in my writing, gifted me with the best possible education and who will forever serve as the most glamorous muse one could hope for. I love you across oceans and beyond the sky, Mom.

ACKNOWLEDGMENTS

I could not have imagined during the haze of my month-long struggle with Covid in April of 2020, that I would soon return to a dream from many years ago in which a gorgeous woman in an emerald green gown dove into a Venetian canal and swam away from a murder. It was a photo of the clear waters of Venice under lockdown that revived this dream, and from it, Gia was born. I want to thank the stillness brought on by the pandemic (and my firing from a certain ad agency), which gave me the mental space to create a new world ruled by a sinister queen.

I want to thank my wife, Eva, for listening as I read, often chapter by chapter. Eva, you have been a constant source of love and support through all of life's experiences—be they good or bad. Each day our love grows stronger. May our dream of being rich old ladies together come to pass.

Thank you to Matthew Axe, who graciously offered to art direct the cover. Matthew, I hope that one day soon we will be at the helm of a bold, creative undertaking: on our own television series.

To my ex-wife, Mariel, thank you for all you taught me about marketing and business, and for your encouragement and support in all the years we were together and in all of the years since.

I would lastly like to thank my editor, Amanda. I was very nervous to place my manuscript in your hands, but you did a beautiful job. I know that the readers will appreciate you being their advocate. I love the little bit of extra drama you brought to Gia's story through your thoughtful changes.

* * *

EXCLUSIVES

For access to exclusive excerpts from Jincey's upcoming books and invites to live readings, visit JINCEYLUMPKIN.COM and join the email list.

1

SEPTEMBER 17TH

The rain had stopped, not that it particularly mattered since the water was so high in the streets. A supermoon lit the flooded St. Mark's Square like a silver lake, and also brought with it the mother of all tides, *acqua altissima*, historically the highest of high tides Venice had ever seen. Coastal flooding had done very strange things to the currents in the canals. Really shaken things up in the water, like a bored child with a snow globe. Things stirred deep beneath the Hotel Bauman, too.

Nico came loose from his chains. His cold body floated up and out; the current carried it tenderly along.

In St. Mark's Square, a German tourist—a surfer—had thrown off his shirt and submerged himself in the deep water to do laps. In the lowest part of the square, nearest to the basilica, cafes were flooded halfway to their ceilings. This bearded German put his whole, long-haired head into the dirty water, and twirled his arms about. After a few minutes, he ran into something blubbery. It felt like the skin of a dolphin. He popped his head up and screamed.

Finally, fifteen days after disappearing, Nicolás Ángel Fernández had been found.

2

SEPTEMBER 2ND

In a dark corner of the canal, Gia sat on the curved wooden edge of her Riva doing what most locals did during the Venice Film Festival: She observed celebrities. Mega-yachts littered the Grand Canal—no doubt there were many billions in global currencies floating on the water.

She was not a star-struck teen. On the contrary, she'd crossed paths with her fair share of the glitterati on the floors of her casinos and in the VIP rooms of her clubs in Paris and Berlin and Monte Carlo. Gia preferred the shadows, though. On this particular evening, she was staked out for one particular star, Nicolás Ángel Fernández, her lover.

Nico was scheduled for the red carpet at five o'clock, a prime slot for maximum exposure to the paparazzi. His handlers would make sure he hit every mark and, then, that he would be smuggled out of the theater's side door just as the lights went down. He couldn't stand the sight of his own famous face on the screen. Never mind that he'd attained "Sexiest Man Alive" status several times over. He didn't even like to see himself on directors' monitors. The lack of vanity, the self-loathing, it was all part of his appeal. He preferred, instead, to look at Gia. Her deep brown hair, nearly waist long. Her pearly skin. She was almost fifty, but he didn't know that—almost no one did. Those fortunate enough to meet her assumed that she was a rich woman in her late twenties or thirties. Her beauty defied logic, except that it didn't.

The two had met a year ago in a tunnel underneath her club in Buenos Aires. He was escaping his pop star girlfriend *du jour*, Jessica Joyce, and her entourage. Gia found him on his own, head against a concrete wall, on the verge of a panic attack. She touched his shoulder and asked if he was all right. He balled up his fists and shook his head.

"Please," she said, "come with me."

She put her hand around his right fist and led him down the hallway to a small office, covered in black velvet wallpaper. She gestured for him to sit, and he collapsed, head in his hands, onto a leather sofa. She opened up a cabinet to reveal a desk and from inside that desk, she extracted a small bottle of pills. She passed him one with a bottle of Pellegrino.

"I don't take drugs," he whispered.

"This is valerian root."

"What's that?"

"It is sort of like melatonin, all-natural," she explained.

He exhaled deeply and downed the pill. "I'm sorry," he said. "This is really embarrassing. I hate crowds."

"Funny choice for a career you made," Gia said.

"Terrible."

"You will start to feel the effects in about ten minutes. What if I tell you a story until then?"

He furrowed his big, black eyebrows at her.

"What," she asked, "you do not like fairy tales?"

"You're a little weird," he replied with a half-laugh.

"The best people are."

That made him think.

"True." He paused for a moment and then agreed, "Fine, tell me your story."

"Lean back on the sofa and close your eyes."

He burrowed himself into the corner of the sofa, resting his head on the soft wall.

"Once upon a time, there was a ship captain..." she began. Nico opened one eye, squinting at her. "*Tsk, tsk,*" she chided. "Naughty boys never get what they want, do they?" He resigned himself and fully relaxed, finally. She continued, "The captain stood at the helm of his bright blue boat and steered past the white cliffs of an island. The sun beat down, baking the crew. They had run out of water the day before. Rain was like a sweet memory from childhood. That summer had been cruel and hot. They dropped anchor and prayed to find freshwater on this dry-looking island."

She slid from the club chair over to the couch and eased in beside him. He turned his head to look at her. He sensed sadness in her almond eyes.

"Who are you?" he asked. "Where did you even come from?"

She laughed silently and smiled a little. "Some people say that the world is destroyed... that the oceans have claimed the land, and that we are all living in a simulation like the Matrix. Do you believe that?"

"If that's true," he said, "I'm sending the coder a fortune in bitcoin." He reached out for her heart-shaped face and took it into his big palm. She leaned in, their faces almost touching. He could already feel her lips on his, but he looked away.

"I have to go," he sighed. "Someone's waiting for me up there. I'm sorry." He pried himself off the sofa and stared at the door. He took a timid step forward. "I wish I could stay."

"Wishes live in fairy tales," Gia whispered, stopping him in his tracks. "So, if you want something," she said, "you should always take it."

"Fuck." He turned around to find Gia perched at the edge of the sofa peering at him, daring him on. "Please," he said, voice trembling, "give me ten minutes? I'll come right back."

She shrugged.

"Please."

"Just fucking kiss me," she commanded. "I know you want to."

He kneeled in front of her. She grabbed his face this time. She kissed him softly, then pulled away. She traced his lips with two fingers and pushed them inside. Her mouth followed and then her tongue. They made love in that small office while his girlfriend sang a coked-up, impromptu set with a famous DJ upstairs.

After their first time together, Nico flew to Gia, or she to him, *rendezvousing* at varied locations around the globe. Despite her high-profile businesses, she took every precaution to maintain anonymity. When he wanted to go public with their relationship, she flatly told him no, that she was an intensely private person and didn't want the press hounding them.

Plus, she suggested, was it not better for his career to maintain the illusion of being single? Did that not sell more magazine covers, get more likes on Instagram?

He agreed, but in interviews, whenever those blonde female reporters would ask him the dreaded question, "Are you seeing anyone special?" he'd have to smile through a pang in his heart. He never felt Gia was his, not really.

And so, as they were set to celebrate a year together on that unseasonably chilly September evening in Venice, Nico, as usual, had to argue with his agent and press squad about not attending the festival after-parties *and* about being on his own without security, particularly during a big event like the film festival. He escaped nonetheless.

In a shadowy corner of the canal, Nico waved to Gia, signaling her over. She motored close to him and scooped him up.

Off they went.

She turned into an obscure, narrow canal and angled through empty boats tied against pilings.

"Where are we going?" he asked. "Are you taking me to that little restaurant I love?"

"No, I have a surprise for you."

He knew better than to ask anything more. He loved her mysterious ways. She took a left into an even smaller waterway and turned off the engine.

"Pass me the big oar from under the back, please."

Nico lifted his seat and reached underneath. She took the paddle from him and used it to maneuver the boat down the tiny canal. Finally, they floated under a small bridge and Gia lowered the anchor. With the new moon in the sky, the water looked black. Flickering on the current was the tiniest light from a bar down the way, a light so small it looked like a singular bulb from a Christmas tree.

"What's my surprise?" Nico inquired, smiling.

"Come here," Gia purred, pulling him in for a kiss. She gripped her hand around the hair at the nape of his neck and yanked it back hard. He moaned with delicious pain. She kissed him below his ear, and licked him, moving her tongue under his lightly-stubbled chin, biting his throat. His body was tense with wanting her. She leaned back and ran her free hand over his face and onto his neck. And then, in one smooth motion, she sliced his throat with the sharp gills in her forearm.

Nico's eyes flashed with hot pain, and he tried to scream but was only able to gurgle sloppy moans. Gia kept her eyes trained on him and felt her pulse quicken with elation as she watched his last moments. He began to stumble, and she pulled him into her, locking him in a deadly embrace. As the blood drained from his body, she held his head on her silk slip dress, resting his cheek against her breasts. His blood soaked through the fabric and wet her nipples. She felt the warm liquid pooling onto her chest, and she nearly orgasmed.

When his body fell limp, she pulled him with her into the water. Her legs swam fast, and then became slower as her scales came in. Toting him through the water was light work once she had her tail to propel her. She turned down the familiar path toward the Hotel Bauman and, when she arrived, dipped into a crevice, dove deep, and tied him up in her graveyard with all of the others.

3

SEPTEMBER 3RD

I n the murky, brackish Rio di San Moisè, Gia ran her hand along the waving grass at the bottom of the canal. Above her, gondolas bobbed like starving baby whales. She'd knotted her blood-stained silk dress at the waist. Her tail, opalescent and strong, whipped through the water like the sharpest knife, leaving barely a ripple.

There was no need to rush. She'd traversed these waterways thousands of times. She loved the scenic route of the zig-zagged streams more than the open water of the larger canals. Gia rounded the bend and swam slowly to her palazzo on the Rio di Cannaregio. At the bottom of her house, deep in the water, she opened a secret hatch that connected to her pool. Inside, she let herself float on the top of the pool, arms open wide. Moroccan lamps filled the room with six-hundred warm yellow stars.

She'd go back for her boat and dock it before the world woke up.

The following day around lunchtime, she walked on two legs, like everyone else, through winding streets and over bridges to a teeny shop that flooded with even the shortest of high tides. Past the peppermint-striped pole, she poked her head in on Vittore.

"*Ciao, Methusalamme!*"

Vittore had discovered what he thought was a most elegant solution to raise the floor of his barbershop and prevent it from further destruction: He'd bought fifteen claw-foot tubs from a wholesaler and simply balanced large sheets of wood atop of them; that way, when the *acqua alta* came, all he had to do was empty the room of the planks and let the bathtubs fill with water. He'd always say, with his hands flailing in the air, "Anyway, Venice is nothing but the inside of a toilet!"

Gia balanced on the tiered risers that led to the very noisy wooden floor above. Anyone over average height would need to sort of fold into themselves to stand up in the space, but it was not a problem for Vittore. He'd battled scoliosis for years, and now the old man was bent like a soggy noodle. Gia craned her head to the side and then plopped down in his barber chair. The ceiling and walls were wallpapered with vintage Coca-Cola signs. Apparently, Vittore had nailed one or two of the signs up for a little panache, and then, first to his amusement and later to his chagrin, customers brought him Coke memorabilia from everywhere. There were tin signs in dozens of languages, with all manner of happy people smiling at you, letting you know that any old problem ya have could be solved with an ice-cold bottle of black sugar-water.

"Want to cut my hair?" Gia asked, smiling.

"*Si, tesoro mio,*" he replied, reaching a bony hand toward his electric razor. "Today, for you, I shave only the very top of your head! It is beautiful, like... like a Franciscan monk!"

Gia laughed and said, "Absolutely, a wonderful look. Please do this for me." Vittore put down the clippers and instead placed his hands into two Stim-U-Lax machines, laying them on her shoulders. "*Amore,*" she continued, her voice vibrating like Katherine Hepburn at the end of her life, "please, can we eat? I am starving."

"Seafood!"

"*Methusalamme,* you know very well that I do not eat seafood."

"And you call yourself *Veneziani.* Ha!"

He switched off the massagers. Vittore and Gia scuttled together across three bridges to their lunch spot. The owner brought them two Aperol Spritz, a bottle of water, and their regular orders.

"*Tesoro mio*," Vittore started, "tell me, when are you going to make a very old man happy?"

Gia glared at him over a salad-stuffed fork.

"When, please, when are you going to find a nice man and make a baby, huh? Can you even make a baby at fifty? I do not know! Do not miss your time like this sad barber, rotting here in a Disney park. I have only you to take care of me a little—and that is thanks to our Father in the sky and to *your* father Luca for that. Believe me, believe me, getting grey, grey, grey and going little by little to dust by yourself, no, this is not a life for you, *bella*. Find a man, please! When?"

"Honestly, Vittore, you are like an annoying grandfather. Every time you start with this."

"Oh, Gia, but that I could be a grandfather! This is exactly what I mean. Do I need to be a ghost, huh? A little white thing flying over a baby crib? I will not live forever. Give me a kind of grandchild."

She exhaled sharply, "What about, 'Gia, how is work? Do the casinos still call the shots?'—we do by the way."

"Work, work! You have so much money. Why work? Why, for what? For more money, more houses. None of that matters. I worry about you, I do. Alone in that big marble house. It will be your coffin, believe me!"

Gia slammed her fist on the table, "*Fermata!*"

Vittore let out a long, sad breath and chewed on a big piece of bread.

"Now," Gia continued, "be a good barber and tell me all the gossip."

His eyes got fiery. "Well, there is a big Spanish movie star... he is like Antonio Banderas, but younger, twenty-seven or something. Anyway, he disappeared last night here in Venice. I am surprised they do not have helicopters buzzing about. Probably they will bring those ugly little drones. They cannot find him anywhere. It is as though he dropped into a hole and disappeared."

4

SEPTEMBER 4TH

"I'm Harper Langley for OTN, and I'm coming to you live from Venice, where just two days ago the Spanish actor and international heartthrob, Nicolás Ángel Fernández, mysteriously vanished."

Across the screen, the news ticker rolled, featuring tweets and Instagram quotes from every celebrity imaginable.

"This is the Lido. It's a glamourous, beach-lined island in the Venetian Lagoon, and it's the last place that Nicolás—or Nico, as his friends, family, and fans lovingly call him—was last seen. Next up, we will speak with actor and director George Cline, who directed the film, 'The Death of Love,' which starred Nico and premiered right here at the Venice Film Festival, the very night Nico disappeared. In these press shots, you can see Nico walking the festival's star-studded red carpet."

Click. Click. Click.

The network edited in the sound of camera flashes as the screen flicked between images of Nico—a solo photo in his tux; a close-up of his wide smile and full lips; his square jaw and his signature light stubble. His hair was slicked back, even though it would normally flop over his face. And it was through that curtain of brown-black hair that he would smolder into the camera lens or at his co-stars, with the deepest green eyes.

"Ironically—perhaps tragically," Harper Langley narrated over the montage that had now switched to candid shots featuring Nico with other stars of the big and small screens, "in 'The Death of Love,' Nico's upcoming film... sorry for the spoilers, folks... he played a possible serial killer who disappears out of the blue. The story follows the search by his family and the police to find him and discover the secret of his disappearance."

The screen cut back to Harper. She stood in a red trench coat, under an umbrella emblazoned on the inside with a step-and-repeat pattern of the OTN logo. Hard, loud rain beat down in the background. Beside her, under a black umbrella was a very troubled-looking George Cline, megawatt smile conspicuously absent.

Harper kicked things off. "The man beside me needs no introduction. He's one of Hollywood's most glowing golden boys—"

"I'm over 60. I think we can all say that I'm a man by now?" Cline quipped, his grey eyebrows arching upward.

"Of course," Harper continued, completely unphased. "George, you've been heavily involved in the search efforts for Nico. Can you share any details with us?"

"Sure, first, if anyone has *any* information about Nico's disappearance, please share it with us at FindNico.com. No love letters, please. This is very serious, and we're dedicated to locating him and bringing him back to his family."

"George," Harper leaned in with her OTN mic, "there are some people who say, 'Maybe this is a kidnapping?' How would you respond to that?"

"Look, the police are investigating every angle. I couldn't—and wouldn't—speak to that kind of rumor. We've been searching on land and by water, checking security footage... everything, looking for any signs that might lead us to him."

"Do you think this could have been a suicide? Some say Nico was depressed."

"Again, Harper," Cline said, mouth tight, "I am not giving

credence to any kind of rumors. I'd like to encourage people to visit FindNico.com if they are able to aid in the search." A short redhead entered the frame and started tugging on Cline's arm. "Thank you for your time, Harper." And with that, he walked off-screen.

Harper raised her eyebrows and said flatly, straight to camera, "I wonder what his wife Amalia would say to that?" Network theme music trumpeted. "We'll be back with Nico's sister after the break to hear the latest from his family. I'm Harper Langley, and you're watching OTN, Our Truth Network, the *only* source for simple truth in this complicated world."

5

SEPTEMBER 5TH

G ia closed up the house and locked every shutter before climbing aboard her sleek speed boat. The wooden vessel, while practically brand new, looked vintage. Its soft-top cover glided over Gia's head with a clean, electronic hum. She steered through thick rain toward Marco Polo airport, with only a small black Hermès Kelly bag in the passenger seat. After pulling into her VIP boat slip, she sauntered to her jet, obscured from prying eyes by an ordinary black umbrella.

It was not until she was above the black storm clouds that she truly began to relax. Her demeanor prior to that, with the jet captain and the flight attendant, had been cool and aloof as usual, but it was an effort to appear so calm. She'd informed the flight attendant that she would not be needing anything on the two-hour trip to London. So, he sat in the front of the plane, in case the captain had any requirements. Gia was alone, on the other side of the curtain in the cream-colored cabin, resting in a suede recliner. She liked being alone, almost more than anything else.

The scene in Venice had become too frenzied. If the city had been busy during the festival, everything was three times as hectic now. Gia felt suffocated. They may as well have projected Nico's face over the city like the Bat-Signal. Therefore, it was better for her to leave town.

When she arrived at her apartment in London, Gia poured herself a glass of Kentucky bourbon on the rocks—the cheap stuff, which in her opinion, was the best. This was maybe the one time in history when London was sunny while Venice got soaked. She slid the terrace's huge glass doors into their pockets and invited fresh air into the space. Whisky in hand, she gazed out over the top of Harrods to Hyde Park. Kensington Palace sat on the horizon to the west, and Gia pondered where the Queen might be today and whether the old woman ever drank a strong whisky, or if it was tea all day, every day. Surely the Queen endured situations that called for stiff spirits?

Gia placed her nearly-empty glass on the Carrara marble that encased her bath. She drew steaming hot water from the tap and poured in the contents of a cylinder of French sea salt, as well as several drops of rose oil. She pressed a button that transitioned the window from opaque to clear, so that she might be able to spy on the Duke and Duchess a little longer. Sinking into the bath, Gia stared out across the city as her tail came in scale by scale. The transformation from skin to scale tickled at first, and afterward had the intensely satisfying sensation of an itch that had scratched itself. She laid back, her tail swaying softly in the bathwater. Legs were fine, and hers were long and strong—good legs, if such a thing exists—but her tail... her tail was part of her soul. It's what linked her to generations of myth- ical creatures through millennia. Man came from ape. Man, by nature, was competitive and clumsy and impulsive. Mermaid, however, had evolved in a completely different way. Certainly the sea had its brutality, but there was also much cooperation and an alien beauty that Man would never understand. The sea is in constant motion, while being on land is deceptive. The world itself changes all the time, but when you're on bedrock, you feel that time stands still, as if the planet's not moving, as if you're the center of the fucking universe—and you're not. Many of the mermaids back in the colony were of the opinion that climate change was the ocean's revenge, and that the days of Man were nearing their inevitable and welcome end.

6

JUNE 1969

C obalt blue paint splashed over the top of the sailboat's mast. Luca descended to the crow's nest and dipped the fat brush again in the paint can. Thirsty work, painting was. Luca felt quite pleased with himself as he took a drink of water.

"Do not fall from there!" Vittore called out from the edge of the shipyard, hauling two giant cans of paint with ease. Slender, tall, and blonde, Vittore was all muscle. Luca felt the warmth of Vittore's big smile from far away.

"Ah!" Luca shouted back. "And where have you been all day, you lazy son of a bitch?"

"Nowhere special..." Vittore said as he approached the vessel, "just fucking your mother!"

Luca flicked the wet paintbrush at Vittore. "Always the funny one. What bounty have you brought for us?"

"Behold..." Vittore replied, popping open one of the pails with the back of a hammer, "for you, my prince, I bring you the blood of your enemies! Ruby red, for you to trod upon."

"Very nice, very nice. I suppose you, *fannullone*, are going to help me paint the deck with this so-called enemy blood?"

"My Father in the sky! Do you hear this? My friend Luca here wants me not only to bargain but also to break my back. Do you know how many haircuts and shaves I had to trade to get this paint? My hands will fall off!"

Luca pouted, "Oh, poor baby of mine. I guess you should probably stay here in Venice to rest instead of sailing to Greece with me."

"Fine, fine. Pass me a paintbrush."

They worked for hours until the sun laid down to sleep. Later, Luca's mother fed them a sensible dinner, and they drank wine and cracked jokes, plotting their voyage for the thousandth time.

Francesca, Luca's mother, stood behind the men in the kitchen, washing dishes, and listening to their dreams.

"Vittore," she sighed dramatically, "you better bring my son home to me in one piece!" She'd been unable to have more babies, so even though he was already grown, she kept Luca very close. She would have preferred for her son to stay home and keep on rowing his gondola like he did every day.

Vittore stood up and put both hands on Francesca's shoulders, massaging them. He laid his head on one of them and tipped toward her so their temples touched.

"I would die first before letting anything happen to Luca," he whispered.

She knew inside that he meant it. All three of Vittore's brothers had died in the war. His life was spared only because he had been a baby. Little Luca, his best friend, ten years his junior, was all he had.

Luca snapped his cloth napkin on Vittore's butt. "Get off my mother, you perverse animal!"

"Ha!" Vittore cried. "Can I help it if she loves me more than you?"

"That is a lie, Vittore Cantalupi!" Francesca protested. "Now, hand me those empty wine glasses and get out of here, both of you."

In a month's time, the sailboat was ready. Francesca brought a large basket of special treats to the shipyard: jam she had made and bottled, hard cheeses, and dried meats. It was enough food to get them through a few days of sailing at least. She waved goodbye, smiling through her sadness, and lingered on the pier long after the men had blinked away into the horizon toward the Greek Islands.

7

"These numbers do not add up, Kosta," Gia commented suspiciously as she clicked through spreadsheets at the computer in the office of her London nightclub. Standing to make her departure, she added, "I am going to go have a few drinks, and by the time I come back, I want to see the profits from July and August. Line by line, yes?"

"Come on, cousin, I would never do you wrong," defended Kostas as he leaned back, heavy against the wall. He rubbed a gold cross around his neck with his wide thumb.

"I will be upstairs," Gia advised, turning on her heel and leaving.

In the club, Gia nestled into a corner banquette. A cocktail waitress passed her a menu and said, "Bottle service only." The server had no idea who Gia was, which was the goal: invisibility. Gia ordered a £1200 bottle of whiskey that would have cost £65 in a shop down the lane.

"Do not bring any sparklers or fireworks or whatever," Gia said. "And no mixers, just ice."

The club was outfitted to look like the belly of a ship. From a perch above the bar, a fifteen-meter-long, wooden mermaid judged patrons through her glassy eyes. Gia's cousin certainly had a sense of humor putting a huge mermaid up like that.

Gia turned her attention once again back to her cousin. Kostas was so hairy on top, she found it shocking that his tail wasn't also matted with fur. He'd always been the most thick-headed of her cousins. Maybe it would have been better for her to transfer him to the Amalfi Coast or even to Venice—to keep an eye on him. She shuffled her Greek relatives around her casinos and bars like a master magician, and anywhere she put them, they minted gold. Except for Kostas.

Three glasses in, Gia was pleased to see that the place had gotten very busy. Hers was one of the last clubs in London where people still danced. Everywhere else, it seemed that people just shouted at each other over cocktails and pints of beer.

Gia dissected the crowd and estimated the amount of coin they'd shell out in pursuit of a good time. There were the Zero-Heroes, men and women who came with empty wallets, looking to get picked up. They tended to have the shortest dresses or tightest jeans. There were clusters of friends—guys and girls—hoping to meet someone the old-fashioned way, not by swiping on an app. And then there were the Sharks—people like Gia.

She spotted a handful of these individuals. They had money to burn but were cautious with their interactions. Sharks had no problem coming to a bar or a club alone. They had plenty of confidence to bite when they saw a dish tasty enough.

"Hi," spoke a man with an American accent over Gia's shoulder. She turned her head.

"*Ciao.*"

"Italian," he smiled with his eyes, which were big, blue, and round.

"American?" she asked.

"Yeah." He glanced around the room and sipped slowly from a glass. He was tall and muscular, built like a Hemsworth. Hot.

"Lawyer?"

"Worse," he groaned, "banker."

"*Tsk. Tsk.* Imagine, a capitalist in a place like this."

"Sad state of affairs," he said, finishing his drink. "I have to agree."

"What are you drinking?" Gia asked.

He looked down at the table, to her bottle. "I'll have some of that."

"Oh, will you?" she laughed. She put her hand out for his glass, and he gave it to her. She began to fill it. "Here?" she asked, squinting up at him through the glass. He rolled his pointer finger to say, a little more. She kept pouring, and he kept rolling his finger.

"Mercy," he said, finally, and she handed the glass back to him. "Mind if I sit?"

She cocked her head at him. He sat.

"Zeus," he said.

"Hmm?"

"Odd name for a club." He sat back and crossed one leg over his knee. He really looked like a man's man, with his arm propped over the top of the banquette, observing everything. Big Dick Energy. She glanced down while he wasn't looking. The view did not disappoint. She would have already gone in for a nice juicy nibble if she were dealing with anyone else, but this American was also a Shark. She'd need to wait and see if she would draw first blood.

"Come here often?" she asked.

He studied her eyes and said, "I think you can do better than that."

She shook her head and scrunched her nose. He never broke eye contact.

"I..."

"Yes?" he inquired, angling his head a bit.

She opened her mouth to speak but could not think of one thing to say. Quite uncharacteristic.

"I live upstairs," he said.

"Perfect. I would love to see your flat."

He laughed and took her hand.

The elevator was lined with leather like a Chesterfield sofa. The ceiling was antique mirror. He passed a keycard and pressed PH without looking her way. They didn't speak at all on the ride up. It wasn't awkward though. There was a strong spark between them, and the fuse was long. She guessed that watching it burn down might be just as fun as feeling it explode.

The door opened into the apartment, which was an extraordinarily lofty studio, all glass. Double height glass walls; cathedral ceiling, also glass. There was a large bed in the center of the room, and beyond that, a clear, pristine cube that housed a large shower and a stainless steel bath.

"Not bad," she remarked.

"Right?" he winked at her. "I do all right."

"My place is not terrible either," she replied.

"Oh? You're already inviting me over?"

She let out a breathy scoff. "Shameless!"

He led her over to the window, and they looked down on London. He came very close to her. "Do you want..." he brushed the hair off her shoulder, and her Cartier earring dangled, twisting. "Do you want a drink?" he whispered in her ear.

"No."

He pressed her body against the glass and kissed her neck. She pushed off the wall and against him to turn around and kiss him, but he thrust his hips into her to hold her in place. And between his legs, he was hard.

"Ahhh," she moaned, unsteadily.

His hand was on her thigh and then up her skirt. "What's your name?" he whispered, as his hand slipped inside her. It felt so good she didn't speak for a moment. His other hand was on her breast, and she felt distracted. "Your name?" he groaned.

"Ah, ah... it is Gia."

"I want to fuck you, Gia." He picked her up and carried her to the bed. Opening the drawer of his bedside table, he grabbed a condom, ripped it open, and fucked her hard until he came. Then he went down on her and returned the favor. They laid together afterward, both staring up into the sky at the growing, crescent moon.

"Not bad," Gia said.

"Right?" He repeated, as before. Then, he looked over at her and kissed her. When he decided to climb under the sheets, he brought her with him, drawing her near. Gia snuggled into his chest as he pressed a button and the whole apartment went dark.

8

The anchored yacht pitched in the sea, see-sawing more intensely by the hour. Clouds obscured any starlight, and the heavens were empty of the moon. The sea was as black as morning coffee.

Marina was below deck in the stateroom, as she had been for hours. Upstairs, the men had drunk all the Metaxa and were now into the ouzo. They chattered and laughed, not that Marina could understand their English. Adonis had turned quite cold toward her ever since his friends arrived. And because she had fallen deeply in love with him over the summer, his withdrawal was very painful to bear. All she could do was wait for him to come to her.

Low light from several lanterns illuminated the men's table, and conversation became sour when it turned toward Marina.

"You should end things," Adonis's friend said, "before she gets pregnant."

"If she isn't already," another one scoffed.

His buddies didn't really get the attraction. To them, Marina, with her strawberry hair and bluish pale skin, was nothing but a scrawny Greek village girl. Sure, she had a pretty face, but she'd barely spoken a word to them all week, and they found her sulky behavior not the least bit charming. She was very much unlike Adonis's vivacious fiancée back in New York.

Adonis held a swig of ouzo on his tongue until the bitter flavor burned. "I needed her to help me... but not anymore."

"Help with what?" one of the friends snorted.

"Shipwreck."

His friends groaned.

"Huff and puff all you like, but we narrowed the search to one area on the map. I'm going in as soon as the sea settles. You can both scuba down with me."

One friend nodded excitedly, while the other shook his head. "Can't... ear problems, not able to equalize."

"That's a shame," Adonis said, raising his glass. "To chests full of gold and fast women. May we always be blessed with both." They clinked their glasses. Shortly thereafter, the friends went below deck to bed, but Adonis stayed up top, ruminating.

Marina took this opportunity to tiptoe upstairs.

"*Agápi mou*, come with me," Marina said softly in Greek.

Adonis spoke back to her in his mother tongue. "Not tired."

She slipped into the booth next to him, but he stood up and lumbered portside, teetering on the edge. She rushed to him and hugged his waist to keep him from falling overboard. He shoved her off, though, feeling disgusted with himself for even starting this ridiculous liaison. In that moment, Adonis was hit with a shocking premonition that he would never be rid of her—that he would somehow be condemned to roaming the seafloor with her forever, never finding the treasure he had dreamed of since he was small. Worse, he had the vision that she would lock him down there with octopus arms, like a Kraken. Beastly thoughts.

Adonis scowled at her and reached out to snake his strong hands around her tiny neck. He squeezed. The things he had to do just to protect himself. He let his anger and self-loathing flow into her. When her eyes finally fluttered shut, he tossed her girlish body into the night sea. He lifted the anchor, powered up the engine, flipped on the searchlight, and drove a safe distance away.

9

SEPTEMBER 7TH

There was the sound of a sizzle and the scraping of metal against metal. When Gia woke up, she was hit with the aroma of melted butter. Soft light flooded in from behind the bed, on the other side of the elevator shaft. The spacious apartment around her was dark, and because it was so dark, it felt cozy. The sheets smelled of whisky and sex and the Shark's cologne—rich with cedar and sage and leather. In the distance, something was dropped into a pan and hissed. Gia lingered a moment, her nose on his pillow, languishing naked and remembering every aching detail of the night before.

Finally, she arose and walked in the direction of the delicious scents like a little cartoon doggie following a meal. On the far side of the elevator bank was a kitchen, which opened onto a terraced, proper garden, trimmed hedges and all. The Shark was in a t-shirt and cashmere sweatpants, cooking an omelet over a six-burner stove. She tiptoed softly, but he saw her from the corner of his eye, and slammed the spatula down with a clang, whirling around and snatching her up. She wrapped her legs around his waist and kissed him deeply. And he stood there, holding her in his arms for a moment.

"I like you naked in the morning," he said, placing her down and then flipping the omelet.

She frowned. "You have too many clothes on."

"Sustenance. Eat first, fuck later."

They both burst into laughter.

"Chef?" Her voice was a little higher than normal. "Ah... what is your name?"

He plated the omelet and put it on a bistro table for her. "Cameron," he replied.

"Cameron." She said his name as if it was a new word she'd never heard before in a foreign language, like it was the first word she heard after living feral with wolves. She sat on a plexiglass chair and stared down at the omelet. This was all very enchanting, dizzying, and made her feel a little queasy, like when one has eaten too many sweets. She exhaled in halting breaths.

Cameron placed another omelet across from Gia's.

"Robe?" he inquired.

She nodded, yes.

He disappeared behind the wall and came back with a soft cotton one that smelled like him. She wrapped it around herself, tucking it in. It hung off her shoulder. She looked every bit like a model in a lifestyle catalog advertising "Enticing Gifts for Him."

The whole thing felt like a scene in a movie, not something that was really happening to her. And she realized that in her forty-nine years on Earth, she had never felt off-balance in this way before. It was a bit like teetering on top of a very thin pole and seeing life functioning below as before, only with a miniature table, a tiny, cute omelet, and this man, Cameron, like a Ken doll. Very strange. Maybe he wasn't like the others.

He sensed from her silence that perhaps she was quite hungover, and he filled a glass of water for her from the tap. She sipped it and smiled to herself about Americans and their damned tap water.

"It is Monday," she thought but said it aloud.

"Mmm-hmm."

"Do you not need to go to a trading floor or yell at someone or something?"

"Nope," he replied. Gia narrowed her eyes, confused. "It's a bank holiday. American Labor Day."

"Oh." She bit into the omelet, finding it light and fluffy. It had mushrooms and sundried tomatoes and very fresh chives, and it tasted like a salty little cloud. "Ahhh, yummmmm."

He chuckled. "What if we spend the day together?" His question didn't sound like a question as much as it did a statement of fact or a verdict handed down from an appeals court judge. In other words, his offer wasn't entirely optional.

And Gia discovered that there really was no good reason to say no. "Yes... yes, I... I think I would like that quite a lot, actually."

They finished breakfast and then showered together. Water flowed in a continuous sheet from the steel panels in the ceiling, and they marveled at London on a rare sunny morning. At one point she took the soap bar and washed his chest. He became very hard, so she knelt down on the tile floor and grabbed onto his cock with two hands. She peered up at him, pouting, and said, "What can we do about this, huh?"

She took him in her mouth, and he moaned. She stayed there until she swallowed his sweet brine and he was soft again. They kissed until their lips hurt. Afterward, they had a lot of trouble getting into clothes.

* * *

CAMERON PRESSED the elevator button for the ground floor.

"Before we go," Gia said, "I need to stop by Zeus." This caused him to raise one eyebrow.

"It is mine," she explained. He was still confused. "The club, I own it."

"Ohhhhh..."

They stopped by the office to find that Kostas wasn't there. However, he'd affixed a sticky note to the computer. In Greek it read, *I need a little more time.* Her cousin really was a slippery little fucker. She decided at that moment that it was time for her to move Kostas to Venice soon, because he clearly needed additional... let's call it, training.

Cameron and Gia took a car from Shoreditch to her place. When they walked into her apartment, Cameron clicked his tongue and said, "Not bad."

"Right?" Gia winked at him.

"Might I get a tour of the palace?"

She kissed his lips. "But of course."

Her apartment was immaculate, colorful, and very feminine. Blue sofa in the double-height living room, mid-century armchairs in orange and pink, and a large Kehinde Wiley portrait of a kid in basketball shorts over the hearth. A Kusama gourd crouched in one corner. At the top of the spiral staircase, on a long wall, were a collection of about eighteen large self-portraits of Andrea Mary Marshall in various stages of undress. Cameron paused in front of one of the photographs of Marshall naked, grinding on a tire swing.

"Hmm." He made a light attempt to observe as an art critic might.

In Gia's room, he sat on the bed and watched her get dressed. To tease him she tried on several sets of lingerie. He liked this game, so he kept inventing excuses as to why she should try on a different set, such as, "Eh... much too fuckable. Hmm... maybe something more see-through?" When she emerged wearing a long green silk charmeuse dressing gown from Agent Provocateur, he whistled, "Definitely covers too much." She slowly untied the belt with one hand and revealed a bra, in sleek satin and a wasp-waist corset with a matching pair of panties and a garter belt. Then she let the robe drop to the floor.

He balled his hand up and bit his knuckle, nodding. She sauntered over to him in her stilettos and outlined the inside of his calf with the heel. He reached out to grab her, but she backed up.

"*Tsk. Tsk.*" From behind her back she pulled a riding crop, and she playfully rapped him on the inside of his thigh. He inhaled through his teeth.

Dragging the whip along his legs, Gia tapped him very gently two or three times in his crotch. She drew the crop out and up to his face, where she popped him on his cheek.

He gave her a mean stare and wrestled the whip from her hand.

"Come here." He pulled her to his lap and placed his hands on her corset, directing her body to lay over his knees. He drew a line up her leg from her ankle, over the top of the pinstripe of the stockings she wore. The curved edge of the leather scratched, especially behind her knee, and it felt like he was drawing on her skin with a pencil. He tapped her between her legs as she had done to him, except he did it a bit harder and only in one specific spot. She gasped whenever the crop struck against her.

"Good girl," he said as he tugged her hair back. "Open your mouth."

She did.

He stroked his thumb on her tongue and then put the end of the crop on it until it was wet. Then he struck her ass over her panties three times, hard. Her breasts were between his legs, and she could feel from how hard he was that he was enjoying himself very much.

Cameron then put the crop down on the bed and slipped his fingers past her panties. He rubbed her with two fingers and felt how wet she was, so he dipped in and out, making her moan. She moved her hips against his hand as he twisted her hair around his other hand, yanking her backward anytime he felt she might be finished.

This made her very excited, and she came before she wanted to.

* * *

THEY TWISTED along the rocky paths in Hyde Park. The roses were celebrating their last hoorah of the year. The air was warm and the sun soft. Half of London seemed to be out, as though they'd all called in sick to enjoy the streak of good weather. Gia stayed mostly quiet and Cameron seemed to be soaking it all up. He walked with his head tilted toward the sky and often closed his eyes. She held onto his arm and led the way.

At the Huntress Fountain, they stopped. Water drizzled past the plinth holding the bronze Diana, and dripped lightly into the greenish pool below. As always, Diana's sculpted hands gripped the bow with ease—a steady huntress she was, confident about striking her prey. The tip of the arrow, with its thick pyramid, was pointed directly at Cameron. Gia smirked at the statue. *Not so fast, Diana,* she thought. *He's my prey.*

"What's got you smiling?" Cameron asked, taking Gia's hand.

"Daydreams."

"Ah," he pulled her closer, "so I'm already in your head."

She squared her eyes with his. "Something like that."

They took a seat across from the fountain.

"I want to know about you, Gia. Tell me, who are you?"

Gia scanned the landscape. Cameron really had a way of putting her on the spot, though she was beginning to feel more settled in herself as the day wore on.

"Who am I..." where to begin? For her, the getting-to-know-you section was always a delicate juncture in the courting process. Reveal too much, and you lose your edge. Reveal too little, and men feel insecure. In her experience, men liked to top from the bottom, to feel they were in control by allowing her to take control. But she knew it was different with Cameron. He wasn't a wounded creature. He didn't appear to suffer from a lack of self-confidence. By all accounts, he seemed to be quite well-adjusted, bearing all the hallmarks of a well-loved man who'd lived an easy life, so the road ahead with him was not at all clear.

He broke the silence with a chuckle. "Why don't we start with the easy stuff," he suggested, "and perhaps, if I'm not *prying* too much, you might tell me a bit about the club?"

She stared blankly ahead.

"Hmmm..." Cameron looked at her as though he were diagnosing her. "Okay, something even simpler then. How about your last name?"

She narrowed her eyes and wrinkled her nose to tease him. "It is Acquaviva."

"Gia Acquaviva," he commented, sort of whispering her name. "Gia Acquaviva. God, that's beautiful. Perfect, really, for you."

"Why do you say that?"

He leaned in and whispered in her ear as he'd done the night before. "Rolls off the tongue." He pushed her hair away and bit her neck. She lost her breath for a moment.

"His mother is still holding onto hope," Harper Langley confirmed, speaking to her viewing public, "but, sadly, the search for Nicolás Ángel Fernández has turned up no firm leads."

The angry sky dumped endless water over the city, and each day, the boats rose. Harper's black Wellingtons reached her knees, and the miserable water was ankle-high. Harper hated Venice. She felt like a swan fighting myriad stinky ducks for the same piece of bread. Her umbrella hung oppressively over her blonde head, and she yearned to be on a bone-dry beach with a frilly cocktail—not that she was one who took vacations.

"It's Nico's twenty-eighth birthday," she said to the camera. "Tonight, friends, fans, and family will hold a candlelight vigil in his honor. OTN will be broadcasting live from St. Mark's Square, and I will be joined by Nico's mother and sister."

Harper couldn't care less about Nico. The only silver lining for her was that reporting about him broke up monotonous election coverage and stories of missing or murdered pregnant women. The ratings on Nico were top-of-the-clouds high. Frankly, it was actually a little surprising to her that a conservative audience like OTN's had taken to the story of a missing Spanish actor. Then again, the powerful pull of liberal Hollywood should never be underestimated. And also, Nico's mother was very religious, and she cried a lot.

11

It was once again grey in London, sunshine evaporated. Gia sat on Cameron's bed, watching raindrops race down the outside of his glass walls. Plans for horseback riding and dinner out had been abandoned in favor of a home-cooked meal. While Cameron sautéed something in the kitchen, Gia snooped in the drawers attached to the low headboard. Inside were neatly organized black leather trays for his keys, wallet, phone, watch, and a remote.

A row of buttons on the table controlled all the apartment's functions. Gia pushed the button on the bottom, and a TV rose from a small ledge at the end of the bed. She turned the sound down and flipped through the channels. Reruns of *The Golden Girls* and *Graham Norton*, endless commercials, and then, a buffet of news channels.

A ticker at the bottom of the screen read, *Birthday Vigil for Nicolás Ángel Fernández*. Gia's heart skipped and she increased the volume ever so slightly, scooting closer to the television.

Floating platforms and small boats filled St.Mark's Square. The camera panned the crowd, and something like ten-thousand black umbrellas glowed from below by candlelight.

Happy birthday, amore, Gia thought. *What a way to celebrate.*

She imagined the scene not as a congregation of people but as a giant, gothic birthday cake, a cake with black icing that she could tread through, and inside, blood-red layers. Sobbing fans held photos of her dead lover and signs that announced messages such as *We love you, Nico!* and *Justice for Nico.*

On a well-lit, covered platform, Harper Langley stood in front of a clear podium in a red raincoat and addressed the audience. "Good evening, it is with great sadness that OTN brings you live coverage of this, the candlelight vigil for Nicolás Ángel Fernández. Nico has been missing for ten days. Tonight, we celebrate his life and send out our prayers for his safe return. I am humbled by the strength of the two women here on this stage with me tonight, Veronica and Paula Fernández, Nico's mother and sister. I welcome Veronica, who will be offering some words to the public and to her son. Everyone, I give you Veronica."

A statuesque woman in her early fifties walked to the podium, leaning on the arm of her daughter. The woman's hair was dark brown like Nico's and done up into a French twist. Gia recognized Veronica from photos she'd seen of her in Nico's apartment in Madrid. Nico had very much wanted Gia to come with him to Alicante for Christmas. He told her about his parents' raisin farm, and how his mother had taken over the operations when his father passed away fifteen years ago. Veronica was apparently not only a beauty but industrious as well.

"Please," she spoke shakily into the microphone, "a prayer." She crossed herself and lowered her head. "Heavenly Father, and gracious Father, we lift our hearts to You. Most loving Father, You are the source of our hope. You are the maker of heaven and earth. Today, Lord, we cry out to You, we beg You—"

Veronica's voice cracked, and tears poured down her cheeks. She took a moment to compose herself and began again, "Lord, we ask You to return to us my son, our brother, our hero Nicolás. Second Corinthians Verse 1:3 says, 'Blessed be the God and Father of our Lord Jesus Christ, the Father of mercies and God of all comfort.' We ask that the Holy Spirit embrace us with love and give us the courage to trust in Your will. In the name of Your son, Jesus Christ, we thank You for Your everlasting mercies. Amen."

She stepped back, and Paula came forward. Paula's eyes shone with fire. "Thank you, Mama—that was lovely. However, we cannot rely on prayers alone." Paula looked directly into the camera, and Gia felt as if the young woman were looking straight into her soul. "I know that you are out there. You have information about what has happened to my brother. Find it within yourself to bring him back to us..." Paula squeezed her eyes tight for a second and then continued. "And if, God forbid, you have done something to him, have the decency and the courage to face the truth and come forward."

Inside, Gia scoffed. *That is never going to happen, beautiful. Not ever.*

Gia was so absorbed in watching the vigil that she didn't notice Cameron standing behind her.

"Ahem, TV off, please. I hate the news... and I don't watch my sister's show, ever." He reached for the remote but Gia snatched it away.

"What are you saying?" Gia snapped at him.

"That's my sister on TV. Gimme." He tried to wrestle the remote away from her hand.

"Wait, your sister is *Harper Langley?*"

He frowned.

"Hold on." Gia shook her head in disbelief. "So, that means... OTN is your parents' network?" Gia had always done her absolute best to avoid the media—and she tried to calculate the pros and the cons of this new development. For a second, she considered leaving Cameron's apartment right then, running from him and closing the door on the threat of media exposure. But then, she realized, with Cameron on her side she might be able to wrangle some additional control over the escalating situation surrounding Nico. *Maybe I can win his sister over,* Gia mused. Such an alliance might prove very helpful, particularly given the unusual circumstances of Harper poking around Venice for Nico.

"Please," Cameron asked, "can we turn off the TV? I just said I don't like the news."

"Why did you not tell me Royce Langley is your father?"

"It's been a problem in the past."

Gia abruptly turned off the television and frowned. "I am not that sort of person."

"What are you talking about?" Cameron snapped back, the volume of his voice rising.

"I am not someone who goes after a man for his money. I have my own."

"Obviously!" he agreed. "But that's not what I meant."

She crossed her arms.

He exhaled sharply. "We're different—"

"Different?" she shouted. "Who is different? What is that supposed to mean?"

"Gia," Cameron continued, he was very annoyed now, "don't cut me off like that."

"Excuse me, I will speak in whatever manner pleases me."

He groaned. "You know what? *Fine.*"

They both sat in silence for quite some time, until he finally gave up and spoke first. "Look, my family is *obsessed* with the news. It's their entire life. I hate that."

Gia stared at him.

He shrugged. "I haven't seen my sister since last year. She's constantly on location. My parents completely disappear into this divisive, sensationalist bullshit."

"You do not exactly stop working at half-five."

"So what?"

"You are being a little hypocritical, a little... judgmental."

"No." He turned to the other side of the bed. "You just don't get it. You don't know my family."

Neither of them spoke for a moment.

Gia broke the silence this time. "I would like to meet your sister."

"Huh?"

"Harper *is* in Venice... and I happen to know *someone* who has a very nice house there." Dead silence. "My friend in Venice also has a *very* beautiful little boat for exploring the canals..."

No reaction.

"This individual even has a private jet to fly us there..."

He perked up. "You have a jet?"

"Mmhmm." She smiled at him with her lips closed.

"Ohhhh."

She tickled him under his arms. "What do you think?" she asked.

He sulked for a moment longer. "I'll go on one condition: I get to fuck you on the plane."

"Maybe you will... or maybe you will not."

12

G reek winds slapped the boat's sails about. Vittore steered, expertly shouting orders to Luca regarding which ropes to pull. The men navigated the violent waves aptly, after all, they were practically born with sea legs—Vittore's father having been a sailor and Luca's a gondolier like him. Their love for the sea was equaled by their respect for it, and to it, they pledged their fates.

Luca scanned the milky surges, keeping an eye out for rocks. Studying nautical maps in the middle of the jolting tide was not possible with only the two of them. Then, as a wave crested in the distance, Luca spied something trapped inside it. The thing rolled and rolled until it splashed against the boat. It was a very large fish-tail, shining blue. The other end of the fish suddenly appeared through the foam... but it wasn't a fish at all. It was a woman. Thinking he must be hallucinating, Luca was brought to reality as the body rapped against the hull, carried along by it. He tossed out a net, snared the form, and with all his strength, heaved on the ropes until the mermaid tumbled aboard.

13

I t was already after midnight, but Gia was determined to finish. She examined row after row of spreadsheets, scrutinizing the ledger for any inconsistencies. Kostas hovered over her shoulder like a pesky mosquito. Bass thumped and rocked the walls of Zeus, but the noise didn't bother her. After all, loud music meant money.

"For God's sake," she yelled at Kostas in Greek, "sit down." She was reviewing the daily automated reports from the tills. "You are missing a week in July. Where is it?"

Kostas fiddled with his cross, as usual. "Computers were down."

"Did you notify IT?"

"Uh," he looked up at the ceiling like he was trying very hard to remember something that was just out of reach. "No, we didn't... my friend finally fixed it."

"Your friend?" Gia said, narrowing her eyes. "That is not our protocol."

"The club was busy, Gia."

She pursed her lips and continued combing through the books. A line-item kept appearing on the spreadsheet for "Other Expenses."

"What is this?" she asked, pointing to a blinking cell in the spreadsheet.

Kostas shook his head like he didn't understand.

"*Other* expenses?" she questioned. "Other expenses like what, exactly? I want to see your receipt logs."

"Oh, um, sure." He scooted the computer toward him and clicked open a different program, pulling up a messy folder of poorly photographed receipts. Some were for amounts that were rather high —and those receipts just happened to be particularly blurry.

"What the fuck is all this, Kosta?"

"Normal shit. Just delivery expenses and napkins and things like that."

"First of all," she said, "those items should be clearly delineated with the appropriate budget codes. And second, this receipt here, it is a duplicate. This other one, it is for five-thousand pounds. No one charges that much in delivery fees."

She glared at him, but he feigned innocence.

"You are fucking stealing from me. It is obvious. Are you stupid? *Do you think I am stupid?* I do not know what I am more angry about... the fact that you cooked the books or the fact that you did such a shit job of it."

"I—I really don't understand what you mean."

"Shut the fuck up. Honestly, just shut up. This is the final straw. I am transferring you. Get your shit in order, Kosta. Clean your apartment out for the next manager, get these books into a state resembling accuracy. You are going to Venice to work under Yiannis."

"Work under Yiannis? He's younger than me! Gia, come on! After everything I've done here? You could never have opened this bar without me. I renovated it—"

"You did, yes. And you went over budget, which I never mentioned to you."

"Zeus is one of the best clubs in town. Everyone says so. It's because of me! I get it packed in here every night of the week!"

"Right," Gia snorted, "do you not think that any of our other cousins can come in here and do exactly what you do?"

"No, I don't."

"Kosta, that is a joke. You are completely replaceable. You will see that. I am finished with this conversation. You are going to Venice as soon as I can arrange it."

"No, I'm not."

"Excuse me?"

"I won't go. I'm not working for Yiannis."

She got very close to his face, so close that he could feel her hot breath on his cheeks. "Do you want to go back to Greece? Is that what you are implying?"

"I was... I was thinking of opening a bar here."

"Aha! So that is the reason you were stealing from me. Fuck you, Kosta. You know I am not going to let you do that. Your options are Greece, where you will live under the thumb of our grandparents, or Venice. Your choice."

Above them, the throbbing music came to a stop.

Gia scowled. "What is going on up there?"

Kostas threw his hands up and waved them erratically, shrugging. "You just said that I'm not in charge here anymore! If you're so smart, then you figure it out!"

Gia whipped around toward the door and rushed upstairs to find the club-goers glued to their cell phone screens as the DJ began speaking over the mic, "Hey bartender, pour one out for Nico. I'm gonna lay down this Jessica Joyce joint for him. Nico, buddy, this one's for you!"

Through the speakers, synth drums pounded over violins. A deep, raspy voice rapped and then crooned a toxic lovesong. Classic Jessica Joyce. She had a face like Rihanna and a voice like Toni Braxton, but what everyone really loved about her was that she had the arrogance of Drake.

Gia pulled up a news app on her phone and discovered that sweet Nico was no longer under the Hotel Bauman where she'd left him.

14

SEPTEMBER 17TH

"For anyone just now tuning in, there has been a major break in the case that has been baffling the police here in Venice, Italy, for weeks. The body of Nicolás Ángel Fernández has been found."

Harper stood in St. Mark's Square, beside her was a skinny guy with a shaggy beard and a man bun.

"Just after midnight, this man, Jens, a German tourist, found Nico's body in the floodwaters that covered this piazza. If you will notice, the entire area has been cordoned off by police. Jens, tell us, did you recognize Nico's face when you came upon his body?"

The hippie guy winced, and in a thick accent said, "The face was so swollen... horrible, horrible... his neck was open and so red... it looked like animals had eaten at him." He covered his eyes as if trying to blot out the image.

"A very traumatic thing to see, no doubt." Harper patted Jens on the shoulder and dismissed him. Then she turned back to the camera. "There is CCTV footage of Jens discovering the body. Roll the tape please."

In grainy footage, Nico's bloated corpse drifted into the wide frame. Jens, splashing around, was totally unaware as he unintentionally beelined toward a most gruesome collision.

Ticking along the bottom of the screen were tweets and press statements from world leaders including the presidents of Spain and the United States, as well as Hollywood stars. All sent condolences and messages of grief over the loss of what they called a "modern-day icon."

* * *

.

15

Cameron was late. Gia scrolled and read through story after story that populated her news feed, sifting through every word of reportage for anything that might implicate her in Nico's murder. She fiddled with the button on her seat, reclining and then popping up again, unable to find a comfortable position. The flight attendant returned to check on her and offer her a drink, and she told him this time that, yes, she'd have a whisky. He brought a heavy tumbler to her along with some crunchy wasabi things to snack on, which she handed back to him and told him not to serve again because she did not care at all for wasabi. Besides, wasabi reminded her of sushi, and she had about as much interest in eating fish as humans did in eating large apes.

Her phone pinged. It was Kostas. His message read, *Sorry to hear about your boyfriend.*

Alarmed, she texted him back, *What are you talking about?*

He responded, *Nico... you must be heartbroken,* followed by several broken-heart emojis.

Gia wracked her brain trying to figure out how Kostas could have known about Nico. She'd only ever brought Nico to Zeus once, and that had been during a time when Kostas was away.

She tapped out a response on her phone, *You are obviously confused.*

Gia stared at the screen for several minutes. Little dots appeared several times, indicating that he was typing, but then they disappeared without providing a message.

Normally she was so good at tying up every loose end.

Had she let something slip? And if so, what was it?

She worried that she had rushed things. With all her other victims, she took her time. However, Nico had really pressured her all summer about going public with their relationship, and she hated that. His fawning attention felt like a heavy arm across her body, holding her down. Circling the net and never getting caught was what excited her. She loved spotting her prey, stringing them along, and then plotting every delicious move up until the end. It excited her even now, thinking about her final kiss with Nico and the rush she felt as she tore through the muscles in his neck. The memories made her heart race.

What Nico most wanted, she thought, was for Hollywood to swallow them both up. He wanted a shield and desired to hold her hand in front of crowds and thank her in awards speeches. She envisioned him selling their wedding photos to a media outlet to raise money for charity. Ultimately, he had become unbearable. She hadn't really wanted to send him off so soon, but he had to go.

Now, the same kibble-hungry packs who had commoditized his life were fattening themselves on his bones. There's nothing like a murder mystery to whip up a profitable frenzy, after all. One article she read said that Vegas bookies were laying odds on suspects; the favorable bet seemed to be on Jessica Joyce.

Outside, Cameron tapped his way up the jet's air-stairs, singing Justin Bieber's *Sorry* extremely loudly. He tossed monogrammed luggage to the side and snapped his way down the aisle with knees bent, like he was doing a very, very bad Michael Jackson impersonation while he crooned. He took her hand and pulled her up to grind on her. As he finished the lyrics in the chorus, he dipped her backward and then kissed her. "Sorry I'm late," he said, finally talking and not singing, "you taste delicious. I'd love some whisky, too."

"Gustav," Gia smiled at the flight attendant, "could you please bring a refill for me and one of the same for my American pop star friend?"

"Friend?" Cameron laid a hand over his heart as though he'd been shot, lifted a shaky hand, and looked at it as though it was dripping with blood. He stumbled backward and landed in a chair across from her, resting his pretend-dead head on his shoulder.

"Soldier?" Gia poked at him with her foot, and he just laid there. He was revived only by Gustav bearing alcohol.

"I won't bore you with the details of why I was late," Cameron said, downing a few gulps.

"I appreciate that." She tipped her fresh glass to him, "*Saluti.*" The captain came out to inquire whether Gia was ready to depart, and she said she was.

As the plane ascended, Cameron took in the view of London below. "I've always loved how small everything looks from up here. It reminds me of a train set I spent years collecting. Every birthday my parents would give me a bridge or a town square, a zoo... I dug tracks in the woods and let the train loop for hours..."

"That is very sweet."

"Yeah," he commented, taking a final swig, "you find ways to entertain yourself when you're six and alone." He sat back in his seat. There was nothing more to see out the window except for the dark sky. "Tell me, do you feel like the heroine in a Merchant Ivory movie when you're home?"

She ignored his question and turned her attention back to him, her mind still focused on his last words about being left alone when he was small. Gia found herself curious now about where Cameron came from—and what his childhood had looked like. She had definitely detected something in his voice that she hadn't spotted before, and she realized it was bitterness, anger. She wanted to learn more. "What about Harper? Was she not at home with you?"

"Not until later. I'm older." he sighed, "Sometimes Harper felt more like my daughter than my sister."

"Hmm."

"Now," he said, turning his attention from the past to the present, "it's time for you to make good on your promise." He seemed eager to shake off the bad memories.

"Which was?"

"Mile High Club. Take your panties off," he whispered.

She laughed. "You want them? You take them off."

Gustav was in his folding seat near the captain and not completely out of sight. Gia could have asked him to swing the curtain closed, but she didn't really feel like it. He was discreet; that's why she'd hired him, after all, and why his salary was so high. Cameron snapped off his seatbelt and crawled across the floor to her. He uncrossed her legs and ran his hands up her thighs.

"Lift," he commanded. She did, and he removed her panties and slipped them in his jacket pocket. Her thighs smelled of lavender and rose oil, but deeper, between her legs, her scent was metallic. When Cameron took her in his mouth, he thought that she tasted acidic like lemon verbena, and sweet, too, like the first hit of the finest California kush.

16

S andwiched between a commercial for erectile dysfunction pills and a pro-life ad campaign ad was Harper's interview with Jessica Joyce.

Cue the theme music followed by the OTN logo. In a grand hotel suite, Harper sat opposite Jessica. In the teaser that aired at the top of the hour of the 60-minute-long exclusive, Harper wasted no time tearing into the third-generation entertainer.

"Did you kill Nicolás Ángel Fernández?"

Click, zoom.

Close-up on Jessica's bewildered face—pink hair falling over one teary eye. Then displayed was a photo montage: Jessica and Nico on a beach, walking out of a gym holding yoga mats, posing together at the Grammys. Dark piano keys boomed in the background. The following wide shot: Harper and Jessica again.

Harper leaned in, "Were you angry about the breakup?"

In for a close-up: Jessica biting her lip as the small diamond of her Monroe piercing above her cupid's bow caught the light.

Close-up on Harper: "Is it true that he checked you into rehab?"

Wide shot: Jessica collapsed in sobs, Harper handing her a tissue.

Finally, close-up on Harper in St. Mark's Square. "Stay tuned tonight for my can't-miss exclusive with Nico's ex-girlfriend, pop superstar Jessica Joyce. You're watching OTN, Our Truth Network, your only source for truth in this complicated world."

As she sat across from Jessica, Harper marveled at how far she'd come as a reporter. This interview was a coup, no doubt the fruit of both the years she'd spent building a reputation as a tough but fair journalist and the non-stop days over which she had been covering Nico's story. At this point, Harper had so aligned herself with this case that when people thought of Nico, they thought of Harper's coverage. With the Jessica Joyce interview, Harper imagined that she would cement her spot amidst the greats like Oprah and Barbara Walters. It wasn't like she was delusional... she knew she wasn't going to win a Peabody or anything. An Emmy maybe? That would be nice.

The glam team finished powdering and tweaking Harper and Jessica's hair and popped out of frame just before the camera rolled.

"Thank you so much for sitting down with me, Jessica. I can imagine this is a very difficult time for you."

Jessica nodded and bit her lip to hold back tears.

Harper continued, "Nico was found two days ago. He had been missing for fifteen days. Jessica, why did you wait so long before coming to Venice? Why is it that you are only here now that his body has appeared?"

"I loved Nico," Jessica began. "I still love him. I'm here, I think, because I want to face the truth."

"Is the truth that you killed Nicolás Ángel Fernández?"

"Why do people think that? Of course not!"

"What do you mean, then, when you say you want to face the truth?"

"I didn't want to believe that he was gone."

"Again, Jessica, forgive me, he had been missing for fifteen days, so you must have realized there was a high likelihood he would not return?"

Jessica began to cry, and Harper handed her a tissue.

"I'm still in shock," Jessica said. "I talked to him the day he went missing."

"Really? What was the nature of the call?"

"I was so proud of him. That movie... it was a huge deal. George Cline, Nicole Kidman, Scarlett Johansson... it was the biggest thing he'd ever done. Everyone was saying it was Oscar material. I told him to break a leg."

"But instead his throat was cut."

Jessica opened her eyes wide, astonished.

Harper leaned in, "Jessica, how long were you and Nico together?"

"Not long enough. Three years on and off."

"Is it true you cheated on him, and that's what caused him to break things off?"

Jessica shook her head violently. "He's the one who cheated!" Then she covered her mouth. "I'm so sorry. I didn't mean to say that. I feel so awful right now, and I don't want his mother to feel like I'm speaking badly about him. He was a wonderful man who I loved so much, and—" She wasn't able to talk anymore, because she was crying, and only sad shrieks were coming out of her mouth.

Harper spoke directly to the camera. "Much more from Jessica Joyce after the break."

17

SEPTEMBER 19TH

The media circus in San Marco had pushed tourists from strolling in their normal loops into other, less-frequented sections of the city, like Gia's neighborhood, Cannaregio. It was Gia's desire to blend into the crowd as much as possible, as there was quite a bit of buzz about the murder. She found it fascinating to observe how people responded to what she'd done to Nico. In a hundred languages, tourists and locals alike shared details they'd read on their phones or watched on the news. There were plenty of wild theories and even a subreddit devoted to amateur sleuthing. Tacked to one bridge, Gia glimpsed a press photo of Nico. On the ground below, lay flowers and stuffed animals and letters. Since the location of the murder had not been identified, and therefore not released, people assumed that any place close to the water was fair game for a pop-up memorial.

Flooding was still very bad, so Gia and Cameron weaved through tour groups. Gia had warned Cameron in advance of what to expect, so they both packed wellies. The tourists, on the other hand, had not, so they trudged along wearing plastic booties over their shoes, which extended up to their knees. The booties were sold in the street by merchants, who were making a killing. In many low-lying areas, water was still waist-high, and even the plastic leg coverings didn't help. Gia had never seen Cameron in jeans. He normally had two modes, which comprised of cashmere PJs and tailored suits. As such, Gia admired this other version—"tourist" Cameron. His butt looked round and cute in his jeans, and she couldn't deny how handsome he was as he crossed the bridge leading to Vittore's shop.

"He is going to die," Gia said to Cameron, glowing.

She spotted Vittore emptying buckets of water from his shop. Someone had placed his barbershop chair on the sidewalk for him, and the wide planks of the floor were stacked up against a wall outside. It was a real mess.

Gia yelled at Vittore as they walked up. "*Fai un bagno, vecchio?*" The old man glanced up at her and smiled a toothy grin with his dentures.

"A bath? Ha! Only if you give me the bubbles!"

"I have brought you something that is going to make you very happy."

"Wonderful! A ticket out of this toilet?"

Gia and Cameron both laughed. She gestured to Cameron, showing him off like a prize on a gameshow.

"NO!" The old man's mouth dropped. "It is a mirage." He shuffled to Cameron and put his hands around Cameron's arms, patting up and down. "I feel him..." He stared up at the younger man in amazement. "Ah! So, I am not seeing things... Gia, this is a man!" Vittore's physical comedy bordered on the absurd.

Gia's laughter rang out like sterling silver bells. "Are you happy now, *Methusalamme?*"

"Happy! Ha! Make a baby first, then you will see me happy! Finally, I will be able to die in peace."

He spoke to Cameron in Italian, "And tell me about you, blondie."

Cameron looked to Gia for help, but she didn't translate. Instead, she leveled her gaze at Vittore. "He is American," she said, in English.

"Americano?" Vittore started singing the lyrics to *Tu Vuo' Fa l'Americano* and dancing... as much as an eighty-two-year-old with a crooked spine could dance.

"Alright, that is enough," Gia said, patting Vittore's shoulder. The old man got very quiet.

But then he began singing in an enthusiastic whisper to Cameron. "Rock and roll!"

Cameron laughed hysterically. "It's nice to meet you, Mr. Cantalupi. My name is Cameron." Vittore threw his arms around Cameron's waist and rested his head on his chest. Gia had to move in and pry the old man off Cameron.

"Cameron," Vittore's eyes shined, "I will give you a haircut today!"

Cameron looked at Gia for help, but she just smiled awkwardly and gave an exaggerated shrug.

"Sit, sit." Vittore pulled Cameron's arm and forced him into the barber chair. He then sloshed into and through the store, returning with a comb and a pair of scissors. "Today, I cut only the front of your hair, yes? Then you come back next week, and I do the back!" Cameron chuckled nervously. After a light trim, Vittore brushed the hairs off his shoulders and neck and ushered the young man over to the shop window for a look at his reflection. "See? Now the dog catcher will not take you away from my Gia!"

"Thank you," Cameron said, reaching his hand out for a shake. Vittore gave him another hug instead.

"*Tesoro mio*," Vittore turned to Gia, "how long will you stay in Venice?"

"*Methusalamme*, Cameron is leaving tomorrow, but I am staying several more days to take care of business."

"I make dinner tomorrow night!"

"No, Vittore, we cannot. We are meeting his sister at Cipriani."

Vittore nodded while elbowing Cameron. "Sister, huh? I am single!"

"Enough, enough!" Gia said, pretending to slap Vittore on the arm. "We are off now. We only came by to say hello."

"I love you, *bella*." Vittore hugged Gia very hard. He whispered in her ear quietly, "I am so happy, my daughter." He then hugged Cameron, too. "Do not be a stranger."

Cameron took Gia's hand as they walked away. When they were

around the corner, he reached under her arms and shoved her against the wall to kiss her. She rubbed her hands on his back as they kissed.

"Show me around." He said, between kisses on her neck. "What about a drink and then a gondola ride?"

She grumbled under her breath.

"Come on," he said. "It's fun! I've never been to Venice. I want to live like common people." He winked at her.

"Ughhhh," Gia griped. "I swear, if you start singing that song I am going to ship both you and Vittore off to Broadway so that I can be left alone in peace." This made Cameron explode with laughter. He enjoyed getting on her nerves; it was too easy.

As they strolled along the crowded streets, she pointed out monuments.

"Give me the *real* history," Cameron said, "your history."

A few moments later, they passed an ancient-looking building. "I went to school here as a little girl. There is a playground on the roof."

"Adorable."

On a less-trafficked thoroughfare, they passed a shop. "This is where my *nonna* bought groceries."

"Do you miss your parents?"

"They have been gone a long time."

"How long?" Gia stared off, with an ache in her heart. *Thirty-four years,* she thought. *Feels like a lifetime.*

"Ah... it has been... what is it now? Twenty years?"

"Twenty years?" He said before he stopped walking for a second. "Wait, How old are you?"

"Thirty-five," she lied.

"Impossible."

She shrugged. "I use a lot of expensive moisturizer."

"Hmm," Cameron had a faraway look. "I've never dated anyone my age before."

"Oh, so you like to fuck grandmas then?"

"Very funny. More like barely-legal models." He realized he

sounded like a dick and he winced. "I love that we're the same age. You're not only beautiful, but you're my intellectual equal."

She gave him a sideways glance, "Young girls are smart, too, Cameron."

He grimaced at the reprimand.

They crossed a bridge, passing a crowded gondola stand. "Let's take the boat here," he said. "But first, is there a place to sit down for a drink nearby?"

"Yes, there is one place that is very special to me."

The Hotel Bauman loomed over them. Five stories tall with thick marble walls and a blocky façade, the hotel looked like a chic, minimalistic tomb. As Gia stepped over the threshold, she felt something stir inside her, and a shiver tingled at the nape of her neck before traveling downward and settling between her legs. Her nipples hardened. She and Cameron walked all the way to the back of the hotel, finding a quaint bar that overlooked the Grand Canal. Outside on the terrace was a statue of a crowned woman, extending a torch into the sky. Many meters below them in the dark waters rested her secret collection of bodies.

Thinking of her dead lovers gave her a rush as she snuggled into the loveseat next to Cameron and slid her arm around him, gripping him tightly. She ordered them two Aperol Spritz and stared out at the Grand Canal. A gondola ferried a group of standing Venetians out of eyesight.

"My father was a gondolier," she said, wistfully.

"Did he sing?"

She sighed and smiled. "Beautifully."

Cameron lifted her chin and focused on her eyes. He wore the most tender expression. He held her face like this and kissed her softly. "I want to know everything about you."

She smirked. "That is so American. Relationships need secrets, *amore*."

"Is that right? Do you have secrets?"

She nodded coyly.

"Tell me one."

"You would not believe me," she grinned.

"Tell me about your mom. Was she a fisherwoman or something?"

Gia's face dropped and the light went from her eyes. "I do not want to talk about Mamma." The sudden shift in her energy made Cameron feel as if he'd done something wrong.

"I'm sorry," he said. She didn't reply. Instead, she dragged the orange wedge around the ice in her glass.

He wanted to put his arms around her, but she was a million miles from him, behind an invisible wall. It was unsettling how rapidly her mood had shifted. He wasn't sure what to do.

Later, when they finished their drinks, they wandered through the city's small canals in a gondola that had a carved mermaid at the helm. The gondolier insisted they kiss under every bridge, so they obliged. Singing Dean Martin's *That's Amore*, when the gondolier arrived at the part where the lyrics talk about love and clouds, he yelled to them, "Kiss again, you two lovebirds!"

Gia rested her head on Cameron's shoulder. He liked having her close to him again. She was soft and warm. He sighed with great satisfaction at this picture-perfect moment.

Gia traced Cameron's Adam's apple with one finger. It lifted with each breath he took. The thin blonde hairs at the top of his throat prickled the ridges of her fingerprint. She fought the strong urge to clasp his neck and stop him from breathing. Under her skin, the gills in her forearm ruffled a little, scratching her from the inside in an unpleasant way. She clenched her jaw.

No, she thought, *not this one. He is different from the others. Special.*

Or, at least, she hoped he would be.

18

"Gia, honestly, he's insufferable sometimes," Harper snickered into her Bellini. "You'll learn this about him. For example, he thought he was going to save America by mailing in an absentee ballot for Hillary Clinton." Harper laughed at her own joke as Cameron watched the sunset through a large window, pink clouds turning the lagoon water purple for a few moments.

"Ha, ha, ha," he snorted. "Look who's so high and mighty now. Little known fact, Gia... Harper is a registered Republican who *votes blue* up and down the ticket. Every. Single. Election."

Harper rounded her subtly-injected lips and made ghost noises. "Oooooh, ohhhh! Quick, someone grab a teacup! I think the male feminist is going to cry."

"You're such a bitch." He punched his sister lightly on the arm.

Harper darted her pale blue eyes to Gia. "Enough about this idiot. Tell me about you. Cam says you're from here?"

Gia nodded, taking a few seconds to assess Harper. She recognized within Harper a certain austerity that had been plastered over. Harper diligently telegraphed a very convincing impression of a person with empathy—when really, the opposite was true. Truth be told, these days Harper no longer cared that she *didn't* care. Somehow, Gia intuitively understood this about Harper. In a way, Gia felt as though she were looking in a mirror and wondered if Harper was picking up the same frequency.

For Harper's part, she was exhausted. She'd switched her mind off. What she wanted more than anything was to slink off to her hotel and drop her mask of civility and sink into her deep apathy like a warm bed. Cameron didn't really know his baby sister, because she didn't want him to. Pretending worked well for her. It came easily. She even enjoyed it sometimes.

"I travel quite a bit for work." Even as she spoke, Gia continued her silent probe of Harper. "I do love Venice, though, apart from the flooding and the tourists."

Harper cocked her head to the side, "So, what you're saying is that you actually hate it."

Gia laughed at Harper's little jab, and then Harper laughed to make Gia feel in on the whole thing. Cameron grinned at the two of them. He was very pleased they were getting along so well.

"I knew you'd love each other." He squeezed his sister's hand. "It's really good to see you."

Harper's heart warmed for a millisecond. "Mmmm!" she swallowed a small bite of shrimp. "That reminds me! I have a message for you from Mom. She said 'tell Cam-Cam to call me'."

Gia sensed Harper's true affection for her brother. She also felt that Harper was distracted and realized this was the perfect time to pump her for information.

"Harper, I have been watching your show a bit. I wanted very much to see your interview yesterday, but your brother would not allow it."

Harper shot Cameron a mean glance. "How rude. Thank you for bringing that up, Gia. I'm actually very proud of that piece, not that Cam-Cam cares."

"No news!" Cameron crossed his knife and fork in front of Harper like a vampire hunter. "Evil! Away with you!"

"Please, *amore*, I want to hear about your sister's job. I am interested, even if you are not!"

Harper toasted Gia's glass, "I like this one, Cam!" She and Gia exchanged conspiratorial glances and Harper continued. "My producers and I secured an exclusive with Jessica Joyce."

"Who is that?" Gia asked, knowing full well exactly who Jessica Joyce was. She scooched closer to Harper.

"She's Nico's ex-girlfriend. A big singer. Huge star. Her mom was a model and her dad was a singer in the 90s. Apparently, her grandfather grew up with Jimmy Hendrix and played drums in some other rock band. There are lots of rumors about her, for instance, that she had a hit put out on Nico. But the thing is, I have very good instincts, and she's not a killer. No way."

"Wow, so interesting," Gia commented as she leaned into the back of her chair, slowly, in such a way as to make her movements look one-hundred percent natural, and not as though she was recoiling from a crime scene.

Harper dropped her voice. "Jessica said he was seeing someone."

"Was he really?" Gia locked into a stare with Harper and opened her eyes wide to make Harper think she was in wondrous shock.

"Yes. And she told me off the record that Nico was thinking of reconciling with her but needed to meet up with someone in Venice first."

A zap of jealousy stung Gia's heart. *That little shit.*

Gia gasped. "Who was he seeing?"

"Gia," Harper tapped the edge of her empty champagne flute and flagged down the waiter to order something stronger, "that's exactly what I intend to find out. I've finally been able to get a private meeting with someone high up in the police. The cops here are so tight-lipped and impossible after all the bad press Italy got from the Amanda Knox case. I have a very good feeling about this week. I think a big development is coming, and I'm going to be the one to break it."

The surety in Harper's voice flowed through Gia's veins, freezing them. This was very bad. For the first time ever, Gia was worried about getting caught.

19

AUGUST 1969

A fter the windstorm passed, the sea turned to the sweetest blue and was diamond-clear. Vittore anchored the boat, and the two men marveled over their changed circumstances, feeling like they'd sailed into a dream. For a full day, they had been the lucky hosts to an actual mermaid. Her tail had vanished before their eyes, fading into two stick-like legs. Luca had wrapped the mermaid in a sheet before she awoke, and now she sat on the deck looking like a lesser Greek goddess. She didn't speak a lick of Italian, and the men's Greek was truly abysmal. Luca retrieved his Greek-Italian dictionary from below and attempted to communicate.

"*Peinás?*" he asked, making his hand into a beak and pantomiming the universal sign for eating. The mermaid nodded, in the strange way they'd read about in their tourist books, where Greek people say "yes," but their head goes to the side in a curious manner, as if they are saying "either way is fine for me." It was confusing. Luca scrambled about, gathering up different snack options and a bottle of water. She eagerly accepted a piece of bread and some hard cheese from him.

Vittore stared at the mermaid and then back to Luca, mermaid-

Luca, Luca-mermaid. This was truly the strangest and most wonderful thing that had ever occurred in his thirty years on Earth.

A mermaid?

This got him wondering: If mermaids were real, then were unicorns and fairies real, too? He'd love to meet a fairy. He'd seen *Peter Pan* at the cinema, and even though he was way too old for cartoons at that time, he had been taken with Tinkerbell. He found her rather sexy. He daydreamed about making a discovery like Luca had, only he imagined himself walking in the woods and following a trail of pixie dust to its tiny little maker. If he had his own fairy, he thought, he'd make her fall in love with him, and he'd build her a beautiful dollhouse to live in.

Bringing his thoughts back to the present, he felt as though he and his best friend had sailed through the waves and landed in another world, and now life would never be the same again.

As Luca continued thumbing through the dictionary, he found what he was searching for and introduced himself to the mermaid, who replied and said she was called Marina.

Greek was extremely difficult to understand, so it was frustrating to speak to Marina, but Luca had uncovered endless patience that day. He wanted to know everything about her. Where did she come from? Where was she going? Could he also go? Was she the only mermaid in the world, or were there others? He tried to pace himself so as not to overwhelm the poor creature. Truth be told, his mother had read *The Little Mermaid* to him when he was small and he had loved it. Once, he saw dolphins in the Venetian Lagoon and imagined it was a group of mermaids coming to take him away. He even read *The Odyssey* as a teenager but was dubious of Homer's negative take on sirens. They seemed more like creepy birds. He was certain that mermaids would be gentle creatures, and by God, he was right. This Marina seemed rather perfect to him, like a Titian painting come to life. After all, everyone in Venice knew the strawberry hue of her hair as Titian red. Back in the old days, women in Venice would urinate in a bucket, layout on the rooftops, and drizzle the urine on their brown hair to try and turn it Titian red. It was a disgusting practice, but fashionable nonetheless.

Luca and Vittore, though, didn't speak to each other about their daydreams. They just tried to talk to Marina. Marina, the mermaid. How incredible.

For Marina's part, she really didn't have much experience with humans. Adonis was not only her first relationship but was also her first real interaction with a human.

One of her uncles had left the colony and gone to the mainland to work for a few years. He returned to Santorini with just enough money to buy a small hotel. Her parents weren't crazy about the idea, but Marina begged them to go live on dry land and work for her uncle, which was how she had come into contact with Adonis in the first place.

To be clear, the colony wasn't exactly against humans; it was just that no one had ever seriously considered living and working among them. Man had always been a looming threat to the sea—something one avoided—and mermaids simply preferred to live their lives in secret as they had since ancient times.

However, like her uncle, Marina longed for something more, something different, a bit of adventure. She never imagined that the chilling tales murmured about Man were the truth. But she had discovered that knowledge firsthand now... Man really was the bitter king of the solid ground. Reflecting on her experience with Adonis, Marina considered these two Italians. They seemed nice, but then again, so had Adonis.

Honestly, though, it didn't really matter whether they were nice or not. Marina only had one thing on her mind, and that was revenge.

20

SEPTEMBER 21ST

Vittore's hand trembled as he lifted his espresso. Gia reached out and steadied it for him. At the end of a long day at the barbershop, the old man always struggled to grip things.

"I think I will stay here tonight, *Methusalamme*." Gia glanced around Vittore's kitchen. "I will help you clean up."

"*Si, tesoro mio*. I am in desperate need of a woman's touch in this broken, old shack."

"I do not know why you will not let me buy you a place and set you up with a housekeeper."

He turned his head and waved her away, dismissing her offer.

"Stubborn."

"I do not need fancy things. I know what money does to people. Look what happened to your parents."

Gia winced at the mention—as well as her parents' memory.

"Vittore... you—you remember when..." She struggled to speak and gulped several times to keep her throat from feeling dry. "Um... back then, you told Papa that you would help him, keep his secrets—and Mamma's—always. And h–help... that you would help me, too."

The old man's eyes became milky and glossy with tears. "Always."

"Well, it appears that I, in fact, am in need of your help."

He grabbed both her hands with his and kissed them.

"I did something," she said. Vittore looked at her intently but remained silent. "Something like... what happened before." This admission caused him to drop his eyes to the floor. "I am afraid to tell you more. I do not want you to be implicated if anything happens to me, but the police... I—I think they might find something that would be bad for me. This has never happened to me before, and I am not sure what to do, *Methusalamme*."

He took many heaving breaths before finally raising his eyes to hers. "There is only one thing to do, *tesoro mio*. Tomorrow you must see *La Nonna*."

21

They called her *La Nonna,* The Grandma. She was sixty-seven-years-old and strong. *La Nonna* swam fifty laps a day, and when she had time, she did one hundred. Of course, there wasn't much extra time in her days—free time is not excessive when you are on the mafia's payroll.

Ultimately, she found her nickname quite rude and sexist, as if all a woman is good for is babies and then grandbabies. She did have grandkids, though, five of them, and she loved them. If people wanted to call her *La Nonna*, then so be it, she thought. In some ways it is better to be underestimated; your enemies never see you coming, because they never saw you as a threat in the first place.

Certain circles of a criminal element came from all over Italy and beyond to her office in Rome. She owned a small, inconspicuous space situated above a cookie factory on a quiet, crumbling street. To be fair, everything in Rome was old and crumbling, but suffice to say that the location was benign and nondescript by Italian standards. There was a small alley beside the cookie factory, and her high-profile clients would park in the back and come in that way. The cookie shop itself had long since been "purchased" from the original family. They still operated it, of course, and they were paid well for doing so, but it was better for them not to know what else went into the delivery trucks beside the *biscotti* and *amaretti*. *La Nonna*, of course, had brokered the deal.

Her real name was Donatella Sapienti, and Gia, like all of the other clients, had come to *La Nonna* for her discretion and unparalleled expertise.

"*Allora*," *La Nonna* began, "what is the nature of your visit today?"

"I would like to pay you first," Gia said, eyeing *La Nonna* and trying to judge her character solely from her body language.

"No, first I hear the problems, then we set the terms."

Gia narrowed her gaze, "I am supposed to trust you? Without some kind of agreement in place?"

La Nonna laughed hysterically. "Agreement! This is hilarious. *Agreement*. You think my other clients make agreements? No. The agreement is I do my job well and they do not kill me. Come on, *piccolina*."

Gia exhaled.

"*Bene, allora*." *La Nonna* was losing her patience, as she was wont to do.

"I am having a small problem with my lover."

La Nonna nodded.

"Ah..." Gia hesitated, "you see, he is dead."

"Did you kill him? Do not lie to me."

"Yes."

"*Madonna!*" *La Nonna* leaned her chair back and spoke to the high heavens, directly with God. "They usually never tell the truth. Incredible." She shook her head and made eye contact with Gia again. "When did this happen? Was this in Italy, and if so, where?"

"Venice, a few weeks ago."

"Venice..." *La Nonna*'s face was like a spinning wheel on a computer screen, querying the database, searching in her memory for the information she needed. "Of course," she smiled. "The actor that they found near the basilica."

Gia nodded.

"You slit his throat." *La Nonna* tapped the end of a pencil on her desk. "And you put him in the water. Messy."

Gia pursed her lips. Her methods had never been a problem before.

"Why did his body reappear?"

"The flooding."

"Obviously, the flooding. This is not what I am asking. My question is why did you not take his body somewhere that it would *not* appear again? This is your first time, I assume." A momentary beat of silence followed as she searched Gia's face for either shame or admission—and then she offered her deduction. "Ah, so this is not your first time."

Gia shook her head, no.

"How many times?"

"I would rather not get into that," Gia said, shifting in her chair.

"Fine, we can discuss this later. Where are the other ones? Hopefully, you were more careful."

"They were with him, in the same place."

La Nonna erupted into peals of laughter. "Well, then they certainly cannot stay living there anymore. No, no. It would be highly inconvenient for someone else to float away now." The woman wiped tears from her eyes as she tried to quell her laughter.

"How do you propose that we move them exactly?" Gia snapped, feeling annoyed that her problem was such a laughter-inducing situation.

"The police are not a problem," *La Nonna* replied, simply and with conviction in her voice, once again focused on business.

"And what about the media?"

"Yes, that is a problem." *La Nonna* leaned onto the desk and rested her elbows. "But not one without a solution."

Gia was agitated, and she dug her long nails into her palms.

"You are worried." *La Nonna* observed. "Let me put you at ease. What are you most concerned about?"

"Jail!"

La Nonna clicked her tongue three times: no, no, no. "You are missing the point entirely, *angioletta*. What I do here is to make sure that you are never a suspect."

That was comforting at least. Gia bit her lip. "I might have another problem."

"Is this problem alive or dead?"

"The man I am seeing... his family is in the media. His sister has been in Venice reporting on the case. She is meeting with the police today."

"I told you, the police are not a problem." *La Nonna* opened a drawer in her desk and handed Gia a flip phone encased in plastic. "Keep this phone with you at all times. Whenever I have information or instructions, I will call you here. As for the boyfriend, my advice is do not end things with him."

Gia stashed the burner phone in her purse as they made arrangements for a fee—an obscene one—to be paid. As Gia turned to leave, *La Nonna* shouted to her.

"Thank you for your business, *Signorina Acquaviva*. Now, please, for the next few months, at minimum, try your best not to kill anyone." With that, *La Nonna* exploded into her same hearty laughter and muttered judgmental statements to herself under her breath.

22

They were anchored near Santorini. Twilight shimmered on the water. Luca and Marina were flipping through the Greek-to-Italian dictionary, as they had for several days straight, giggling together, and mumbling clumsy sentences. Vittore fished off the back of the boat and was rewarded with several seabreams. His father would have been proud. He gutted the fish out of sight from Marina; he had noticed that it seemed to really upset her anytime she saw him slaughter his catch. What's more, is that she refused to eat grilled fish like the men and instead subsisted on stale bread and jam.

Vittore lit a fire on a portable stove and the trio sat around it, eating their dinner. Marina was attempting to explain to Luca how and when her tail appeared, as the subject was most fascinating to him. However, he was unable to understand what she meant when she told him that she drank a soup that contained a hormone to help her regulate the functioning of her tail. It was probably better that he didn't understand. It would have ruined the magic for him.

Luca and Marina couldn't take their eyes off each other. Vittore felt like a United Nations observer. He kept his silence and gave them space to discover each other. Vittore dreamed about meeting someone special one day. Maybe a pixie, maybe a handsome sailor. Someone would come along. He was sure he wouldn't be single forever.

"*Psáchno gia navágio,*" Marina said, "*Échei thisavrós.*" Luca asked her to repeat every word so that he could learn what she was saying.

He translated to Vittore. "Marina says... 'I look––no wait, I searched?' Yes, there we are. She says she is looking... for a shipwreck."

Marina nodded. "*Kai o thisavrós.*"

Luca translated, "And the..." He sounded out the next part, "thee-sav-ros," to try and find it in the dictionary. Very difficult thing to do because of Greek's complicated-looking alphabet. He found his way to the "Theta" section and skimmed through the pages. "*Thisavrós!* Found it! It means––"

Luca's jaw dropped.

"What?" Vittore waved with his hands. "The suspense," he said, pretending to faint, "it is too much."

"Treasure. *Thisavrós* means treasure. She's looking for treasure from a shipwreck."

Vittore laughed. "What else can one expect from a mermaid, huh? Do you really think she is under the ocean looking for a bus stop?"

Marina patted Luca on the arm and pointed at him and then pointed to Vittore. "*Pamé mazí.*"

"She is saying, let's go, Vittore," Luca translated.

"*Mazí, mazi,*" Marina said. "Together."

"Treasure!" Luca said, smiling at Vittore. "That is an adventure, no? Adventure is what we dreamed about when we thought of sailing. Should we go?"

Vittore didn't answer right away. He imagined chests of gold coins and remembered his father and all his years on the sea. He thought of pirate ships and again about *Peter Pan* since that story had all the elements: pirates and mermaids and a whole island of treasure. Then he reflected upon King Midas and how the man nearly starved to death because of his Golden Touch. What would riches even mean to him? He had nearly everything he'd ever wanted. Also, the idea of a shipwreck seemed a bit fanciful, but then again, only days before so had the possibility of mermaids.

"Marina," Vittore said, "we will help you find your treasure, but do not trap us at the bottom of the sea."

23

W ater never felt cold to Gia. Perhaps water in the Arctic Circle might, but who knew? Some said reclusive colonies of mermaids lived under the polar ice caps, but to Gia, that was only speculation. Regardless of temperature, however, there was a good chance that anywhere in the world she dove, Gia would survive just fine. September water tickled her naked skin, though. A mesh bag hung across her chest. It made a soft pattern as it wafted through the canal.

When she reached the crevice under the Hotel Bauman, Gia hesitated for a moment. But then, into the cavern she went and down, down, down to the bottom, where they all laid, forever asleep. Her eyes cast a faint glow around her, and she swam to a most holy place; it was an altar cut from stone. On the altar was a box with a bas relief of Christ on the cross. She slid off the top to reveal its contents. Inside were the bones she'd carefully laid to rest so many years ago. She picked up a skull and brought it to her face, kissing it.

"*Ciao, Mamma.*"

She gingerly placed every last piece of her mother into the mesh bag. *La Nonna*'s men would be there soon to dispose of the other bodies. As she swam home, Gia felt like crying, but not a tear dropped.

24

OCTOBER 3RD

A waiter filled the table covered with a striped tablecloth with platters of crudité, focaccia, and grilled cauliflower. Cameron and Gia liked Shoreditch House as well as all of the other Soho House locations for their no-photos-allowed policy and relaxed atmosphere. The couple had zero interest in socializing, except with one another.

The rooftop bar was a short walk from Cameron's apartment and al fresco dining was the thing since this was likely the absolute last chance they would have to sit outside comfortably before winter weather descended on London.

Cam snuggled Gia into his cardigan and kissed her forehead. He felt at ease around her in a way he never had with anyone before. Admittedly, she was always a bit out of reach, but he enjoyed pulling her over to his side. She made endless interesting observations about the world, like a person possessing many more years of experience.

An old soul, as they say.

He loved that she never pressured him for anything—not a commitment, not money, not even affection or time. She was tight-lipped about her businesses, but then, so was every other halfway-decent mogul he'd ever met, and he recalled that his parents used to say that they couldn't get Rupert Murdoch to utter a word regarding any of his dealings.

Cameron often wondered about Gia's net worth, and whether she was in the high eights, nines, or even ten digits. Impossible to say. She wasn't super flashy, didn't shop like crazy, or overspend. Everything about her was elegant and understated.

And the sex?

Forget about it. Best of his life.

For him, Gia was one in a million, possibly one of a kind. He just needed to figure out how to keep her around. It had been nearly a month since he'd met her, and he was already feeling those elusive *forever* vibes.

"How long are you staying?" He asked her, monitoring himself so that he sounded somewhat aloof and not needy.

"I head back on Monday. Venice calls," she answered.

"We should get away together soon."

"We shall see," she said, sipping her wine. "I have a few pressing projects that require my attention."

Thinking to herself, she knew that she first needed to collect Kostas and deposit him with his new babysitter, Yiannis, at her casino in Venice. Then she was determined to observe *La Nonna*'s removal crew from a distance, even though the old woman had specifically told Gia to stay out of Venice for the week.

Gia had decided to fake flight logs and send her jet to Argentina. If necessary, her cousin down there would produce "evidence" of Gia having been in Buenos Aires. It was a solid plan. Of course, Gia would have preferred to stay in London to fuck and laugh the days and nights away, but her long-term personal and financial security were priorities.

"Any news from Harper?" she inquired, keeping her voice light.

Cameron was onto a steak now. He swallowed and said, "She's been texting me more since we met up in Venice."

"How sweet. Is she still there?"

"She said the crew is leaving tomorrow. I guess she's planning to stay for a few more days, you know, Sherlocking. Do you want me to connect you for drinks or something?"

"Oh... unless she is available Monday, I am not free. This week I fly to Buenos Aires."

"Livin' la vida loca," he smiled, making Gia laugh.

"Thank you very, very much for not singing that!"

"Ah! Now that you've challenged me..." he began singing into a hunk of steak on his fork like a mic. When he got to the hook in the chorus, he hovered the fork-mic below her mouth.

Gia sang the missing lyrics somewhat flatly, to placate him.

"That's the spirit, baby!" He took a swig of wine and kissed her.

25

I n June and July, Marina had spent her time leading Adonis around the Aegean Sea in circles. She more or less knew where his beloved shipwreck languished, but she clung to the prospect of more time with him, because she feared, rightly so, that with the sight of so much as one gold coin, he would drop her. She fumed thinking of him, and she scratched an "X" on Vittore's nautical map so hard that she nearly ripped the paper.

Whenever anyone pictures the Greek Islands, no doubt it's the rocky terrain of the *Kiklades*, the Cyclades, that's conjured in the mind's eye. Apart from Santorini, where the boat was now docked, and one other small archipelago, the rest of the "islands" in the Cyclades are actually peaks of the same submerged mountain chain, poking out from the water. Marina explored the porous terrain with her brothers and sisters for years. There were caves—tiny ones and huge ones—and the ridges along the seafloor comprised a topography filled with all kinds of treasures.

The deepest part of the Mediterranean—or so the experts thought—was in the Hellenic Trench. Coined Calypso Deep, and reaching far into the sea, it had a depth of about seventeen Eiffel Towers stacked one atop the other. What the divers, sea captains, and scientists did not know was that a different, deeper trench existed, just to the east of Crete.

The mermaids called the area "Cold Currents." The sea was saltier there, the water heavier, and the tide chaotic. There were folktales of creatures being dragged into a riptide when they approached the area and were sucked into the center of the Earth, never to be seen again. Cold Currents was off-limits for mermaids.

Marina pointed to Cold Currents on the map and the men nodded. She took the dictionary from Luca and began to explain to them what needed to be done.

"Before go," Marina said, in her terribly broken Italian, "there is problem."

The men squinted at her.

"Very bad man," she whispered, "he want also... *thisavrós.* We run, run fast. Be first to *thisavrós.* Understand?"

"Someone else is looking for the treasure, and we need to beat him there. Is that what you're saying?" Luca asked her.

"Yes, bad man."

"But, why are we here in Santorini?"

Marina was pretty sure she understood what Luca was asking. "Find *theíos,*" she responded.

"Uncle?" Luca said, recalling a word he had seen in the "Theta" section of the dictionary.

"Yes. Uncle Stavros." She gestured to the top of a very tall mountain. "Hotel. Uncle Stavros hotel. There."

Luca sighed. "I see. It looks very far away. We should probably leave now."

Marina raised her eyebrows.

Luca pointed at the three of them, "*Pamé mazí.*" Let's go together.

Marina lifted her chin once, sternly. Luca remembered that in Greece that movement meant "no."

"No?" he asked.

"No," she said. "You." She then looked up to the mountain top again and back to Luca. "You go Uncle Stavros hotel."

Luca frowned and made eye contact with Vittore, making a decision. "You stay here with Marina then. I'll be back soon."

Luca started to walk away, but Marina grabbed his arm and cried, "*An deíte ton Adonis, prépei na fýgete.*"

"I don't understand."

She sighed and banged the palm of her hand on her forehead. How could she explain that they were all in danger? "Adonis."

"Adonis," Luca repeated.

"Yes," Marina said. "Very bad man." Then she paused and made a hand signal from the hilltop back to the ship. "Luca, Stavros. Here."

Luca blinked several times, seeking to comprehend what Marina wanted, and said, "I think I understand." With that, he vaulted overboard and hurried up the dock.

There were many paths up the hill, but Luca had no idea where he was going or what he was searching for. Every building looked the same; they all had curved white walls, blue shutters, and cascades of bougainvillea. He snaked up, up the hill until fortune shined upon him: He found a couple speaking Italian.

"*Mi scusi, sto cercando un hotel di proprietà di un uomo di nome Stavros.*" I'm looking for a hotel owned by a man named Stavros.

They chortled and quipped in Italian. "Good luck, son. Every third man you meet here is called Stavros!"

Luca shuffled away, a bit discouraged.

Afternoon was giving way to evening, and at the harbor, Marina and Vittore stood together, staring out at the horizon. Vittore was hardly a quiet person, but, unlike Luca, he hadn't spent the last five days chatting with Marina, stringing Greek words together, so he felt shy for the first time in his life. Every once in a while they would glance at each other and flash an awkward, closed-mouth smile. Finally, Vittore had an idea.

"*Vino!*"

Marina glowed. "*Vino!*"

Vittore was rather pleased with himself for finding a solution and breaking the ice. He fetched a couple of wooden cups and, into them, drained some red wine from a barrel.

"*Saluti,*" he said, toasting her.

"*Geiá sas!*" she replied. Then they both took a gulp.

Two cups later Vittore felt lubricated and ready to chat. "I know you do not understand me, but I feel like a very silly person standing here and drinking in silence. I think, perhaps it is better if I talk and maybe you listen to me?"

Marina understood the words talk and listen, and that was about it, so she simply shrugged her shoulders in agreement.

"Let me tell you about Luca."

"Luca!" Her eyes sparkled.

"Luca is the brother I never had. My brothers were all gone before I was out of diapers. Sometimes Luca, well, feels like a son to me. He is the friend everyone deserves. I do not know a better person. There is no better man than Luca Acquaviva."

Marina's cheeks dimpled, and though she did not understand what Vittore said, she knew the contents of his heart. His love needed no translation.

"It is because of Luca Acquaviva that I became a barber." He made little scissors with his fingers and lifted his hair like he was cutting it. "Chop chop, bye bye!"

Marina bubbled with laughter.

"You see, Luca's father and my father, they were friends also. My mother, she died a long time ago, so I spent many nights eating dinner around the table of Luca's mamma. At school, they sent Luca away from class, because his hair was too long! Many days they did this, but Luca did not go home when this happened. He pretended to be at school, and instead, he spent the day fishing. Finally, after weeks, his teacher brought him home by the ear to his mamma. I was there. The teacher... she was a nun... she was yelling at his mother, Francesca, 'This boy is a disgrace! Why do you not cut his hair? Do you see this? His hair is almost to his chin. He cannot come to school anymore until you cut his hair above the ears!' Father in the sky, he was shaking. The nun left and Francesca cried! She grabbed the scissors, and Luca ran out the door. She looked at me and said, 'Vittore Cantalupi, you go get my son and do not dare come back until his hair is as short as the fuzz on a peach!' I chased that little Luca down the streets and across fifty bridges until I caught him. I said to him, 'Damn you, Luca! Come here and let me cut your hair before the dog catcher takes you away for good.' He sat down by the water and let me trim him up. His black curls floated down the canal like a string of tiny Os."

When Vittore glanced over at Marina, her face had gone pale, and she was trembling. Seeing her like that made Vittore's stomach flop.

"What is it, Marina?" Her eyes had a faraway look in them and Vittore followed her gaze.

"Adonis," she answered, fear in her voice.

She was fixated on a boat that was sailing into the harbor at a good clip.

"The bad man?" Vittore asked, moving his body in front of hers. Her eyes were starting to tear up. "Get down!"

She slid down to the deck of the ship and curled under the lip of the boat's rim. Balled up like a snail, she prayed that he hadn't seen her while Vittore kept watch as Adonis and his two friends tied their yacht to the pier.

Vittore's heart beat out of his chest as he spied Adonis ambling up the same road that Luca had ventured just hours before. Crossing himself and saying a silent prayer for Luca, Vittore studied his watch. If Luca did not return in an hour, Vittore was going after him.

26

OCTOBER 4TH

It was early afternoon when Gia breezed into Zeus. Even though she had in front of her the unpleasant business of dealing with Kostas, she was still feeling high from a long night with Cameron and a leisurely brunch in his apartment. In addition to the sex, dating him was certainly convenient for checking in on the club.

If she didn't have the whole mess with Nico, she almost could have left Kostas to get on with things, albeit while keeping him on a tight enough leash. Unfortunately, circumstances were not in his favor.

As she entered the dimly-lit space, she heard Kostas laughing and speaking in Italian, not Greek. The club was empty and she smelled a stale, minty odor. Making a mental note to have the cleaning crew come and sanitize, Gia found Kostas huddled into a corner banquette near the bar. In front of him sat several bottles of open liquor and an expensive magnum of champagne on ice. Circling him were three men—two meathead-types and one skinny, short guy. Gia's mood instantly soured as she recognized the men as players involved in a drug-smuggling ring. They had once infiltrated the cocktail staff at another one of her clubs and used the waitresses to deal coke, ket, and molly. It took several months for Yiannis to weed out the bad seeds.

Kostas saw Gia and promptly dismissed the men. They downed their drinks quickly and, as they cleared out, each acknowledged Gia with a nod. Once they were out of earshot, Gia started in on Kostas.

"You never fail to disappoint," she sneered.

He was a bit drunk and off-balance.

"Where are your bags, Kosta?" Gia asked. He scratched his head as if confused by what she was saying. "Give me the apartment key," she demanded, holding her hand out. He rustled in the pocket of his too-tight jeans and passed her a jumbled ring full of keys.

"That's everything," he slurred.

"Since I see not a single suitcase, I am assuming you did not pack and that the apartment is a mess. I will send someone to get your things. Time to go. Come on."

Gia didn't even bother to ask about the mafia guys. She had a good idea of why they were there. They always had their feelers out for an easy mark, and Kostas, the dumb fuck that he was, would make the perfect victim.

Once on the plane, Kostas snored three-quarters of the way to Venice. The other portion of the plane ride he drank ouzo, turning to sulking openly when Gia cut him off. When they landed, they walked to her boat. The Riva was parked in its slip as usual, and as they zipped through the choppy water, Kostas leaned over the side of the boat, heaving his lunch into the canal. Gia slowed the throttle as they passed Hotel Bauman. In the Grand Canal, surrounding the hotel were a small barge and a police boat. Her heart jumped. Either *La Nonna's* crew was a day early, or...

Better not to think about the other option.

She hummed to the north and tied her boat to the pier at her casino. Inside, the slots and tables were unusually busy for a Monday afternoon. Cruise ships, monstrous as they were, always brought in lots of tourists who were more than happy to part with their money at a famous Venetian casino.

All around the place, people were doing their best James Bond or

Bond Girl impressions. However, all Gia saw were stacks and stacks of chips.

The Eye was on the third floor of the casino. Yiannis, as usual, was glued to the wall of monitors. He gave her the warmest hug, and they air-kissed on both cheeks.

What a dream it would be if all my cousins were like Yiannis.

"*Koúklaki mou!*" He'd always called her his little doll, or little fish or little mermaid, even though he was twenty years younger.

"So good to see you, Yianni. You have to stop doing such a good job running this place, or I will never have the occasion to stop by." Gia draped herself over an Eames chair as Kostas crumpled onto a stool. Yiannis remained standing. "Kosta, say hello to your cousin."

Kostas glared at Yiannis but didn't speak.

"He has been pouting like this since we left London—when he has not been passed out drunk, that is."

"Ah," Yiannis said, "this is gonna be fun, *trichotós skýlos!* Perk up. We'll have you back in shape soon."

"No one has called me hairy dog since Greece, so you can stop right now."

"Sure, sure, no problem. From now on, I will call you Prince Kosta." Yiannis rubbed Kostas on the shoulder as he spoke.

"Could you lay things out, please, Yianni?" Gia asked.

Yiannis tilted his head to the side to say, yes of course and reached into a drawer for a folder, which he passed to Gia. "I organized everything, receipts in the back. There is a summary of the audit on the first page."

Her eyes bugged. "Fifty thousand! In two months? Good God Kosta, maybe there is hope for you after all." He shrugged. "The deal is this... first, you will pay me back all the money you stole. Yiannis is going to take it out of your salary until we are even. Second, no more mafia friends, and—"

"They're not my friends," Kostas grumbled. "They're my business partners."

Yiannis and Gia sputtered out a laugh. Gia looked Kostas right in the eyes and said, "You do not have business partners, understand? You work for me, or you do not work at all. I already told you, it is this or Greece. This is your last fucking chance, Kosta, and you better not waste it."

Yiannis clucked his tongue. "It is not good when she gets angry, Prince Kosta. Look, Gia, don't worry. I will take good care of him."

"Thank you," she said. "Last thing, Kosta, you listen to everything Yiannis tells you. No back-talk. Nonsense will not be tolerated. Now, I have to run."

She hugged Yiannis again and whispered into his ear that he was the best, and then she slipped out the door. She was several meters down the hall when Kostas grabbed her from behind. She spun around to face him.

He was red and scowling. "I know things about you, Gia. Things my business partners would find *very* interesting. You should learn to treat me with more respect."

She took a step back and blinked cooly. A few breaths calmed her pulse. To Kostas, her face was unreadable, and he shifted back and forth on his feet. He wasn't afraid of her. Well, maybe only a little afraid.

"Hmm," her voice was almost a hum, "and what is it you think you know?"

He wasn't prepared to be called out.

"Y–you, you know... you know what I mean."

"Do I?"

He did nothing except gawp at her.

"Yianni?" she called out down the hallway. Yiannis stuck his head past the door. "Kostas is ready to start his shift now."

Without another word, Yiannis gathered up Kostas and ushered him back into the office. Gia disappeared behind a panel and out into Venice.

* * *

THE TALL CEILINGS in Gia's palazzo boasted ornate carvings in wood and stone. Gia had decorated the house in a Moroccan style, with wedding blankets layered over silk rugs.

At that moment, Harper was curled into a fluffy chair, peering at Gia over a tiny espresso cup. Gia thought that Harper looked remarkably like a hungry cat, round eyes squinted with feline curiosity.

Admittedly, this was a first for Gia; she'd never met the families of the men she dated, let alone hosted a lover's sister in her home. However, everything considered, a private coffee seemed like the most discreet option.

Gia made it a point to never dwell on her failings or shortcomings, but lately, her mind churned with a nagging sense of... self-doubt? She wasn't sure. She was feeling a bit off course since Nico, as though her moves were a bit too improvised and not as strategic as usual—as strategic as they *should* be. Calculated risk was always a big part of the thrill, but what if she had miscalculated?

"How's Cam-Cam?" Harper asked.

"He is driving me crazy, in the best way."

"He's dying to show you off to Mom."

"Oh?"

"Once she gives her stamp of approval on anything, there's no going back."

Gia felt Harper studying her face. Was she searching for micromovements?

Gia took a sip of water. "Harper, you are making me nervous!"

"Don't worry. I'm on your side."

Is she though? Gia wondered.

"I told him to hold his horses. I don't want her to outright reject you just because he's moving at warp speed."

Gia's chest tightened. She calculated the risk in asking Harper about Nico and decided she could pretend convincingly to be naive.

"Ah... so... how are you? Do you have any developments in the big case?"

Harper sighed and threw her head back dramatically. "The police here are *impossible*. But... I was able to find out from a source that they are investigating one specific suspect."

"Really?" Gia's palms went all sweaty and she had to grip her water glass more tightly so that it didn't fall to the floor. "How do they even do that?"

"Don't you watch cop shows?"

"Television is not really my thing—I mean apart from your show, of course."

"Truth be told, I'm still learning how the system works here. The good news is that I have a line out in Madrid, and it's wiggling a bit."

Gia raised her eyebrows.

"My sources there are collecting information," Harper continued.

"About?"

"Gia! I can't spill all my secrets. For all I know, you could be spying on me."

Gia laughed, hoping she didn't sound nervous. "Just a little taste?" she prodded.

Harper smirked. "There's an ex-girlfriend, apparently. Can't tell you anything more, or I'd have to kill you!"

27

NOVEMBER 7TH

C ameron rubbed the small of Gia's back as she leaned over him to look out his side of the helicopter. The water below was deep blue.

"See, it's there." He tapped the glass, pointing out a big yacht below. He kissed her, and she opened her mouth to him.

Between them, in her Hermès bag, her burner phone buzzed. She knew which phone it was because the phone *La Nonna* had given her had a stronger vibration that lasted longer than her personal phone. Cam didn't know the difference.

"Need to get that?"

"No, no. *Amore*, today I am focused only on you."

He smiled with his tongue on his top teeth. "I love the sound of that, baby."

The ship's crew greeted them when they touched down on the helipad. Cameron had planned a two-day jaunt for them. The yacht was charted to hug the Côte d'Azur from Cannes to Monaco. He wasn't interested in sailing a long distance. The goal was simply to give his girl a good time. Shame it wasn't warm enough for swimming. The chef whipped up a delicious meal, and Cam asked the stewards for some privacy. He used a table knife as a champagne saber, and when the cork popped, he yelled, "Happy Anniversary!"

Gia wondered if this was what he did after two months, what was the plan for a year?

"Gia, I think it's pretty clear, but I just wanted to tell you... to express to you... to let you know... how absolutely crazy, madly in love with you I am." He clinked his glass against hers. "No pressure. Don't feel obligated to say it back now. I was exploding. I couldn't hold it in anymore. I fucking love you, baby!"

She grabbed his stubbled cheeks with both hands and kissed him hard. He put his arm around her, and they found a spot on the back of the boat to watch the sunset.

However, Gia drank only a tiny amount of bubbly, because she was feeling queasy.

"*Amore,* do you mind terribly if I lie down for a bit? I need a tiny, tiny disco nap."

He smiled to mask his disappointment, but nonetheless encouraged her, "Yeah, yeah, rest!"

She snuck into the large stateroom and took out the flip phone to ring back *La Nonna.*

"What did I tell you?" *La Nonna* barked.

"Not fond of hellos are you?"

"Do you think this is all a joke, *piccolina*?"

"Pardon me, your attitude toward me is really becoming quite rude. Mind your tone."

"*Allora,* Gia, when I tell you to do something it is because it is best for you. What did I say, ah? I said, 'Answer the phone every time I call.' I said, 'Stay out of Venice.' You did not do that either."

"What are you talking about?"

"I have eyes everywhere, and last month they spotted you in Venice when I told you very clearly not to be around."

"You work for me... you do know that, right?"

La Nonna cackled so loudly that Gia had to hold the phone away from her ear. "How could I forget! You are a really huge headache.

Bene, allora, the reason I am calling is because I have news that is not so good."

"Meaning?"

"My boys in Spain tell me that your boyfriend's sister, the talkative one from television—"

"He only has one sister."

"She was in Madrid today."

Gia looked at the chevron patterned carpet on the floor. It appeared to be pulsating. "And?"

"It seems there is some security footage of you and your ex."

Gia didn't speak.

"Do not worry," *La Nonna* whispered, "we are taking care of it."

"How?"

"Do not ask."

"Are you going to hurt Harper?"

"Gia, did I inquire as to how or why you slaughtered those eleven men we found down in your underwater basement? No, I did not. So, let me do my work, please. Honestly, I am already worried about going to hell, *Signorina Acquaviva*. Do not put me in an early grave. *Madonna!* You will give me a nervous heart attack."

Gia heard Cam creeping down the stairs, so she quickly hung up.

"How are you feeling?" he said, edging in.

Gia looked at him and was suddenly overcome with nausea. She ran to the bathroom and threw up.

28

T wo middle-aged men sat under a lemon-yellow umbrella and argued across the top of a backgammon board. On the white wall behind them, hung a very small sign that read: Stavros Suites.

Luca had located the hotel, and he was grateful, as the light of the day was fading. Without hesitation, he interrupted the men.

"Hello, I am looking for Stavros," he said in Italian.

"Is he expecting you?" one of the men asked, through a salt-and-pepper beard.

"No, but—"

Before he could even begin, a group of young men walked up behind Luca.

"Adonis!" the bearded man sang out.

"Stavros!" Adonis and Stavros hugged and kissed each other on each cheek.

Adonis was handsome and incredibly tanned. He didn't carry the air of a bad guy with his grinning face—at least not to Luca.

"Where's Marina?" Adonis asked, speaking English to Stavros.

"Is she not with you?" Stavros replied. Suddenly, Luca felt sweat gathering under his arms.

"Nah, she came back here two days ago."

Adonis was lying, and Luca knew it. Heat spread across Luca's chest as he struggled to envision what had really happened between Marina and Adonis.

Stavros pulled on his beard. "Odd. I will go to my brother's house now and see if she is there. Why did she return here? Did you argue?"

"No! Of course not. She said she was feeling seasick, tired of being on the yacht... and I get it, kind of wears on you."

Stavros scrunched his face up quizzically and rapped his knuckles against the wall. "Seasick, huh?"

Luca wondered if Stavros was thinking what he was thinking. How could a mermaid get seasick?

"Yeah..." Adonis looked up at the sky as he spoke, "she, um, she beat feet, man."

"Is that so?" The pitch in the man's voice rose.

"Yeah, what a drag. I like her a lot. Woof... women... right fellas?" Adonis gestured his thumb toward his two buddies, and they backed him up.

"Can't live with 'em..." one friend started, "...can't drown 'em!" the other one finished.

Adonis snickered nervously. Luca felt his fist balling, and sweat slipped between his fingers.

"Hmm," Stavros muttered, with a suspicious, yet absent look on his face. "How about this... you playboys have a shower and then we can all go look for Marina together."

Adonis inhaled through his teeth, "Oof, sure wish I could, old man, but we've got to jet early in the morning. I think I finally found the shipwreck, and we are sailing to Crete at sunrise."

Stavros sucked in his cheeks and his beard shifted. He forced a smile and said, "Then I will see you at checkout."

Adonis snapped in the direction of Stavros, winked, and strode inside the hotel.

Stavros had forgotten all about Luca, and he was lost in thought over what to do next. Luca woke him out of his daze.

"*Scussi.*"

"Yes?" Stavros replied in Italian.

Luca scooted in very close and lowered his head. "I know where Marina is. She sent me for you."

"What are you saying?" His voice was hostile.

"We have to go to the harbor right now."

"Who are you exactly?" Stavros bristled. "What is going on here?"

Luca held his hands up, showing his palms. He bit his lip, "Ah, look, Marina and I have been together for the last five days. Adonis is lying. Marina says he is not a good man."

Stavros shook his head a bunch of times as if trying to clear the fog that had enveloped him. "What, what? Five days! Where?!"

"Shhh..." Luca tried to calm him.

Stavros began cursing under his breath in Greek. "Take me to my niece right this instant."

Without further haste, the men jogged down the hill. They carried themselves at a pace that didn't allow them to speak. Vittore met them on the road, close to the harbor.

"Father in the sky!" Vittore shouted. "I was coming to look for you! Adonis is here!"

Luca doubled over, out of breath. "Ah—ah, we know. We... *wooooh*... we saw him."

Stavros grabbed Luca by the shoulders and squeezed hard. "Where is Marina?"

Vittore moved both his hands slowly, like an orchestra conductor, to say simmer down. "Everything is all right. It is all right. She is on our boat. She is just fine. Come and see."

"Marina!" Stavros screamed. "Marina! Come out here!"

"Shhh... please!" Luca whispered intently. "Your voice carries! Adonis might hear us." Stavros ran down the dock and whisper-yelled Marina's name until she whispered back to him in Greek from inside the men's blue boat. Stavros climbed up the rope ladder. Luca and Vittore followed him aboard.

Once on the ship, Stavros began accosting Marina, "*Ba!* Who are these *malakas* and what is going on? Little girl, you must explain everything to me this very moment. I am of half a mind to swim out to your father and mother right now. Tell me, what is going on?"

Marina burst into tears and fell onto her uncle's shoulders. He embraced her tightly until she stopped sobbing. He moved the hair out of her face and caressed her cheek. "*Koukali mou*, please, what happened?"

Marina told him everything. She told him how she'd led Adonis on a wild goose chase just because she loved him, and explained how he'd more or less dumped her once his friends arrived. And then she began shaking violently and crying again, but this time much harder.

"He tried to kill me, Uncle. And he tossed me out into the sea like a piece of trash. Luca found me, and these boys took me onto their ship. They fed me and helped me. Uncle, you cannot imagine. I was so weak. I thought, truly, that I might die."

"Marina, I will kill this man with my own bare hands!"

"Stop, Uncle! No! He is not worth it." She wiped tears away with the back of her hand.

"Then I curse him! I curse him to have much suffering as long as he shall live and I demand from the Gods of the Seas and Sky that his own misery be the cause of his painful death. What a miserable pile of excrement."

He hugged his niece and stroked her hair until they both calmed down.

"Uncle," she said, "I want him to pay for what he did to me."

He widened his eyes at her.

"The treasure is at Cold Currents, Uncle. I want to take it from him."

"No, Marina. No. I would rather let you stab him in the night. We cannot go to that place."

"Please help me do this, Uncle. I can never rest until I do. And you know I cannot stay here. If he finds out I am alive he will kill me dead this time. I have to leave Greece. I need this treasure so that I can start a new life and be safe. You know this is the truth."

Stavros' eyes began to water, and he stamped his feet on the deck and cursed, walking in circles for a moment, kicking at random things on the boat, like coiled ropes and the barrel of wine. He finally came back to her. "Marina, I love you more than my own life. I promised both my brother and your mother that I would keep you safe, and I have failed them. I have failed you. You are right... as much as I hate it, you are. We must leave for Cold Currents tonight. Adonis will sail for Crete tomorrow, so we have to beat him there."

"We need help, Uncle. I believe that the ship is deep in the water."

"Then help you shall have. Stay here. I will return soon."

He was gone for over an hour. When he came back, it was with six of Marina's cousins and a large, stolen motorboat. Her cousins carried thick chains that they often used to fetch things from deep waters.

"Get in," Stavros yelled to Luca and Vittore.

"What about our ship?" Vittore asked, very distressed.

"Your God smiled on you both and blessed you with this new vessel."

"Oh, really? Do you hear this?" Vittore huffed in Luca's direction, arms crossed.

Luca shrugged. "Adventure, my friend, adventure."

Stavros drove for hours into the dark night. When they reached Cold Currents, the boat began to teeter in the heavy surf.

"Drop the anchor," Marina said, "The shipwreck is here. I can feel it."

Marina's cousins secured the chains and tossed them into the water. Then, one by one, they tore off their clothes and dropped into the waves. Luca and Vittore watched the water by the searchlight. Tails flicked in the seafoam. Stavros was last.

He brought Luca to the back of the boat and got next to his ear. "Your name is Luca, yes?" Luca nodded. "Son, if something happens down there, I want you to promise me to take Marina and go. Do not think, just go. Do you swear?"

"I do," Luca replied, solemnly.

Stavros patted him firmly on the back a few times and into the sea he went. Marina paced up and down the boat waiting for her family.

"How can they see down there? It's so dark..." Luca searched the water for any signs.

After a long time—they were not sure how long—two of her cousins surfaced. They swam to the edge of the boat and yelled at Marina, "You were right! It is here. First round coming up!"

They pulled themselves into the boat, tails and all. Luca had absolutely no idea what to expect from a merman. Their tails were thick and veiny like strong muscles and had black scales that glistened like motor oil on hot pavement. Suddenly, though, their tales began to... Luca couldn't even understand what he was seeing... began to dissolve and split in two, leaving two sets of strong, olive-skinned legs on the deck. Something yanked on the chains, and the men hauled them up easily, as though they were reeling in a flimsy jump rope. What appeared then were two additional cousins who were each holding onto a chest filled with greenish-grey coins. The chests were mossy and slippery with underwater goo, and they almost dropped the first chest. Down again, they went. Then another set of cousins came with yet another chest. And another. And another.

It was very quiet for a long time and no one else emerged from the dark depths below. The cousins on the deck told Marina they'd better go down, so they dove back in. The sky was changing. Winds raged. The boat swayed dangerously in the waves. The heavy chains caused the boat to dip violently in one direction.

"We are about to take on water!" Vittore screamed at Luca. They acted swiftly, dropping the chains off the boat. That helped stabilize things enough to avoid capsizing, at least for the moment. While they were working, Marina disrobed and snuck into the sea.

Her thin blue tail was strong, too, but not like her cousins'. She fought against the current as she searched the water for them, eyes lighting the path. The water was devoid of life. The gills in her arms and under her ears swayed as she swam. Finally, she saw them all, grouped together near a gash in the seafloor. She swam nearer. Her cousins formed a chain, thrashing their tails backward from the current to stay in place. The closer she got, the stronger the tide felt. It swirled and she started rolling in a rip current, trying to pull her somewhere unknown. Marina felt disoriented. The cyclone of water kicked up lots of sand, and through wafts of debris, she could see her uncle. He was holding onto the edge of the crevice around which her cousins had gathered. They tried to swim to him to pull him up, but each time they tried, the current batted them away. It was as if there were an invisible hand yanking on her uncle's tail, while another hand swatted the others angrily away. Two of her cousins broke loose from the others and grabbed her. They rolled together on the bottom of the sea and nearly fell into the opening along with her uncle. Marina's cousins took her by the arms and kicked the water with all their might, lifting her up and away. They didn't stop until they hit the surface.

"Let me go!" she screamed. "I want to help! We have to go back down there and get him!"

But it was too late, dawn was breaking. One cousin yelled for Luca's attention, and when Luca saw their faces, he remembered his promise. Marina was howling incoherently as the two mermen dragged her to the boat.

"Help me lift her up, Vittore!" Luca yelled. They grabbed her and held on until she was safe.

The mermen shouted at Marina, "Leave now! Do not look back! Everything will be all right. We will save him!" They ducked into the waves, and Marina tried to jump overboard. However, Vittore held onto her waist, even as she hit him and kicked him all over. Luca lifted the anchor and steered the boat northwest, toward Venice.

29

NOVEMBER 16TH

"I am handling it," *La Nonna* insisted, calmly.

"If you are handling it," Gia screamed into her burner phone, "then why am I watching myself on television right now?"

"There was an oversight," tisked *La Nonna*, sounding unconcerned. "The individual has been reprimanded, as you will see in a text message very shortly. Everything is under control."

"It does not feel like that!"

"*Allora*, the best thing you can do right now is to live your life as if everything is normal."

Gia heard the beep of a keycard at the door. Her security latch clanged.

"I have to go," Gia said quickly.

"Listen and listen well to me, *piccolina*. Do your best not to kill anyone."

La Nonna snickered as Gia hung up.

Cameron knocked, more demanding now. "It's me," he called out.

The burner phone buzzed with a text. There was a photo of a man shot in the head from behind and only the words, *Scuse sincere.*

Sincere apologies. Who the fuck was that dead man? She turned off the phone and slipped it into a drawer.

Turning to open the door, she found that Cameron had the look of an unlucky soldier who'd been ordered to press the button to start a nuclear war. He didn't speak. He walked in and stood silently in the middle of the living room.

"You lied to me." He didn't look at her, and would not meet her eyes. His gaze was intently focused on her wet bar.

She eased into a chair and folded her legs. "No."

"No?" His pale skin blotched, and the room seemed to heat up. "Harper called me this afternoon. Do you know what she said?"

Thank God Harper is even alive, Gia thought, surprised at how much relief she felt.

Gia did her best to be expressionless, to appear as an innocent to Cameron.

He glared at her with rage now. "She has a fucking source who identified you with that actor! They have proof you were romantically involved!"

As his temperature rose, hers dropped.

"Cam—"

"I'm not finished! I *begged* her, Gia. I begged my own sister not to release the information."

"I have to tell you something."

"Good, because I have a lot of questions!"

"I am pregnant."

He stumbled backward. "Wh—I'm sorry... what did you say?"

She rose and opened a mother-of-pearl box that sat on the table. She passed him a pregnancy stick with closed hands. He took it from her in slow motion, held onto the stick, and examined it. The truth was right there in bold pink letters: PREGNANT.

He stumbled around the room, confused, like a man trying to walk on the moon, and finally fumbled his way over to the wet bar. He poured himself four fingers of whisky and drank half of it in a gulp before collapsing onto the chair across from her. The glass coffee table between them may as well have been the size of all oceans combined. Cameron remained quiet for a very long time, so she matched his behavior. What could she even say?

He put his hand over his face and breathed in extremely rapid breaths. As his throat tightened up, the faintest wail escaped from deep inside him. It got louder until he screamed out and slapped his face hard several times. Crying into his palm, the salt from his tears stung his clean-shaven cheeks. After what felt like forever, he laid the little white stick on the table and stared at it.

"We have to go to New York," he croaked.

"New York?"

He was still weeping a bit, and nodded his head despondently. "We have to go to my parents, and we have to go tonight."

She rubbed her temples. "Why?"

"Because, Gia, the only place safe enough to hide from all the beasts is in the belly of the biggest one."

30

NOVEMBER 16TH

Once they boarded the jet, he called Royce and Bronwyn. Cameron's parents were taken aback by the prospect of a sudden visit, but also glad that their son was coming home. As for the Italian girlfriend, that was another matter. They'd already put their best investigator on the case. They were not fond of surprises, so the day's revelation about Gia had not been enjoyed.

Gia had the flight attendant make the sofa into a bed, and when he had finished, she asked him to bring her and Cameron water and two whiskeys. Cameron took his drink and stared out the window into blackness. Admittedly, Gia did not like him sulking like this and decided to try to distract him from his anger with her and change his mood.

She undressed.

Back at the apartment, she had quickly showered after packing and put on some La Perla lingerie. Easing onto the bed beside Cameron, she slid on her stomach, with her rear end in the air, like a kitten. The garter belt caught his attention as she curled up next to him. He was under the sheet, leaning against the back of the bed. Without really meaning to, he had an automatic physical response. The sheet stirred in his lap and lifted.

Gia looked into his blue eyes, to find that they were so sweet with worry. She stroked her hand across the sheet over his lap, but he pushed her away.

"*Amore mio*," she said, rubbing her forehead into his neck.

He didn't respond.

She lowered one bra strap from her shoulder and then the other. Her breasts were propped up in the balconette like eager little children awake past their bedtime, spying on a party. Popping the hook, the bra slid down to her navel. He drank her in with his eyes, not wanting to. Gia traced her nipple with two fingers and felt pleasure tingle to the rest of her body. Her other hand glided across her belly and into her white lace panties. She was wet, and one finger slid in without resistance. Then another. Cameron watched her as she arched her back. He took her in, her light pink lips, delicate nose, her brown eyes closed, her beautiful breasts, and her flat belly. Without thinking, and completely on instinct, he reached out and placed his hot palm on her stomach.

"I'm not going to let anything happen to you or our baby." Then he kissed her in the softest way he ever had, melting into her like chocolate. He slowly pulled her panties down to her ankles and climbed on top of her. She gasped as he moved inside her.

"Open your eyes," he said, and she did. He was crying. "I love you."

31

W hen the motorboat hit a patch of rough waves, the gold coins would sometimes slosh in their chests. Marina heard every metallic clink. To her, the sound was unnaturally loud, like a screeching flock of iron birds descending upon her. What a horrible idea it had been to seek the treasure. Revenge had none of the sweetness she had imagined. She felt bitterly cold and sour in her heart, and she worried constantly about her uncle.

Of course, Luca and Vittore were lovely to her. The men hugged the coast of Greece before running up the back of Italy's leg along the Adriatic. They had to stop frequently for gas, and since they had very little money, the men often had to steal fuel in the middle of the night. All in all, it took about a week to return to Venice.

For Luca's part, though he had no idea what had happened under the water, his heart ached for what Marina must have experienced. In the commotion in Santorini, the men hadn't thought to take much with them from their ship, so he did not have the Greek-Italian dictionary to aid him now in speaking with Marina.

He communicated mostly with his eyes.

From time to time, she let him hold her. When he had her in his arms, he felt as if he needed nothing more from life. There she was, his true-life fairy tale, and he wanted nothing more than to find a permanent place in her heart and kindle a soft fire in it to keep her warm. He resolved to stay patient and let her have the time and space she needed in order to let him in.

Once they arrived in Venice, Vittore departed from the boat to bring Francesca back to her son. When she returned with Vittore, she threw her arms around Luca and thanked the heavens that he was home.

Of course, upon the sight of the new boat and the odd redheaded girl who was currently dressed in Luca's clothing, Francesca had plenty of questions. The men, though, told her it was a very long story, and they were very tired—explanations would have to wait.

So, the four of them waited until nightfall to unload the treasure into a cart and wheel it home. Francesca fixed up a bed for Marina in the living room and prepared a very large meal for the kids. Marina gobbled up the pasta as though she'd never eaten before.

The next morning, Luca only had one thing on his mind.

"Vittore," he said, "what are we going to do with all this gold?"

32

NOVEMBER 17TH

They arrived at the Langley estate in the middle of the night, New York time. Their black Suburban pulled into the *porte-cochère*, and Cameron burst out of the SUV to embrace his mother and father. Bronwyn reached up to her son's face and held it in her palm, smiling with a closed mouth. It seemed like she might cry, and Cameron kissed her on the cheek and pulled her close again. She held him extra tight with her eyes closed.

"Okay, Mom," Cameron said, "I get it, you missed me." Bronwyn chortled a melodic laugh. "This is Gia," Cameron said as he held Gia's hand as she exited the Suburban.

"Well, miss," Royce said in appreciation, his voice deep and glossy, like the wise male lead in an opera, "you are stunning. Please come in. We are very happy to have you here." He rubbed her arm in a reassuring, fatherly way.

Cameron's mother reached out for Gia's hand and squeezed it before going in for a hug. "I could not be more delighted to meet you."

"Enchanted," Gia said, attempting to yield herself to this unwanted invasion of her personal space.

Once inside, they stood around the kitchen for a moment, and

Bronwyn insisted on pouring them some chilled American tap water from a glass pitcher.

"I know you're both exhausted. Let me get you settled."

She set them up in a large guest bedroom upstairs and then headed to sleep herself.

Under the sheets, Cameron held Gia close to him, kissing her head and stroking her arm. "I think we should look at apartments when we get back to London."

"Really?" Gia's chest tightened. Moving in together? That was territory she most certainly was not ready to enter.

"A room for this one," he caressed her tummy. "And maybe," he whispered into her ear now, very faintly, "another room for another baby."

"Mmhmm." Her breath became shallow—all of this felt very fast and rushed—so she brought his hand to her lips and kissed it, just in case he noticed anything was off.

"I love the idea of them in little school outfits..." he sighed with satisfaction.

Who is this person? Gia wondered. *What happened to the Shark I thought he was?*

His verbal efficiency had given way to a new style of speaking: dreaming out loud. Gia was rather unsettled by his change in personality. He didn't feel at all like a Shark anymore. He was a whale now, rising to the surface of the water and spouting out errant streams of nonsense.

In the dark, her eyes dashed around the room frantically. She was very much awake. Cameron nestled into her shoulder, drifting into a warm sleep, and Gia felt the urge to jump from the bed and rush to her plane and take off to... to anywhere, honestly. But instead, she remained motionless, laying there with her man's arm stapled across her.

Her mind raced, churning over possibilities like a geek genius with a Rubik's Cube—except nothing fit together in the right way. She enjoyed spending time with Cameron, but her desire for the thrill of the kill was at times overwhelming. Either way, for the moment, she was stuck with this lover. After hours, she finally fell into an uneasy series of nightmares.

In the morning she put on her face, dabbing a bit of extra concealer under her eyes and flicking on an additional coat of mascara to make herself appear alert. The smell of bread was wafting upstairs, and there were cooking sounds coming from the kitchen. Cameron escorted her downstairs, and they met Royce and Bronwyn at the breakfast table.

"We've taken the day off." Royce poured orange juice into their glasses. "Shall we dive in?" There was a bountiful spread on the table, but Royce was not speaking about breakfast, unfortunately.

Bronwyn cleared her throat, "We had a long talk with Harper this morning—"

"Mom," Cameron said, placing his hand on hers. "We have some news first."

Royce and Bronwyn put down their forks, nearly in unison.

He smiled. "We're expecting," he said.

We are expecting? What is he expecting, exactly? Gia thought bitterly. *I am the pregnant one!*

This terminology annoyed her very much—even more than when a couple announced they're "pregnant."

Is this feminism? Men now take part in the pregnancy as much as the women? Is this not, itself, patriarchal? Can women have anything that belongs only to us? Will Cameron start saying he is having his period, too?

Cameron looked at Gia, beaming as he was not able to read her thoughts. In response, she smiled and kissed him chastely.

Royce and Bronwyn exchanged a glance of wordless communication, in the way people who have known each other for a very long time do, where the slightest arching of brows is a whole language. Bronwyn interpreted Royce's signal with ease.

"How exciting," she said to her son. "This calls for Mimosas. Royce, my darling, please pop a bottle of champagne."

Royce brought a cold bottle from the wine cellar and Bronwyn had the housekeeper dust off the flutes and bring more juice.

"To love," Bronwyn toasted.

"*Saluti*," Gia made firm, non-aggressive eye contact with the elders and clinked glasses.

Bronwyn passed a basket of fresh croissants with salted Irish butter. "Now, there's a bit of business to discuss. Darling?" She kicked it over to Royce.

He coughed. "There is a source," Royce grimaced, "who claims to have... uh... additional footage."

"Of what?" Cameron asked, voice sharp.

Royce hesitated, so Bronwyn jumped in. "It's of an *intimate* nature."

Gia turned her champagne glass nearly upside down, draining the last bit.

Cameron exhaled sharply. "What are you saying? Sex tape? With Nico?" His mother winced. Cam clenched his jaw and bore two holes into Gia.

For her part, she had never participated in a sex tape—not with Nico, not with anyone—nor would she. Where had the tape even come from?

"This is not poss—"

Before Gia could even protest, Bronwyn jumped in, steamrolling her. "We need to get in front of this."

"Exactly," Royce continued. "Admittedly, we got scooped on the details regarding Gia and..." Royce trailed off, clearly feeling very awkward by the looks of his downturned mouth.

Gia tried to fill the dead air, "I never—"

"That poor Nico." Bronwyn interrupted Gia again, without even looking in her direction. Then Bronwyn turned her head toward Cameron. "It's really unfortunate what happened to that man." She exhaled deeply and then darted her eyes to Gia. "Please understand that we do respect your privacy, so do not feel that you need to tell us anything. We have someone very discreet who has been working with us for a long, long time... we think it would be best if you could share the details of your relationship with our friend."

Gia opened her mouth to speak but—

"Mom, no," Cameron interjected. "This is... this is very weird."

Royce sighed. "Son, the world is watching."

"You always say that, Dad."

"Yes, Cam, I do. Because it's true, buddy. In this instance, there's a lot of... what's the word? Appetite... for... uh... blood."

"A fire your network stoked, no doubt!" Cameron said, face reddening. "Raking in those precious ad dollars!"

"My dear," Bronwyn's voice was soft, it was clear she was being careful with her words, "we are trying to help you. We need to insulate you from scandal... and not *just* scandal... darling, the media and the police, the whole machine... if we don't step in... well, sweetheart, it's going to roll right over Gia and crush her into the ground. Do you remember that woman who was accused of killing her child? I think it was in Florida... he was in the trunk of the car I think? Anyway... trust me, it's going to be like that, Cam, but worse. The world is relentless with female killers, even suspected ones. That poor Nico was at the top of his career. One of the highest-paid actors out there, with millions and millions of fans all over the world. They are aching to find *someone, anyone* to project their pain, fear, and anger onto. Do you know what they will say about Gia? That she's a femme fatale, that she slit his throat in the night like Jack the Ripper!"

"Jane the Ripper," Royce said, face grim. "That's got legs." Bronwyn nodded in agreement.

Cameron covered his face with his hands and spoke through them, "This is so toxic. I hate the news."

"Nevertheless," Bronwyn continued, "this is the world we live in, and we have to protect you... and Gia... from it. We can't have your baby born thinking his mother is some kind of *psychopathic serial killer*, for goodness sake."

Gia shifted in her seat and picked at the corner of a croissant, trying to take all the information in. She wasn't sure why they even needed her here for this conversation. Plus, anything she said might get taken the wrong way and make her look bad. There was a Spanish expression Gia had heard once: *Calladita te ves más bonita.* You look prettier when you shut the fuck up. She slathered some strawberry jam on the flaky crust and took a delicate bite.

"Harper is flying in tonight," Bronwyn continued. "For now, we have everything contained. When she arrives, we will sit together and discuss the details of the plan."

Clearly, the Langleys had it all figured out, handled. Suddenly Gia felt that her days of independence and total authorship over her own life had somehow evaporated. Being out of control made her feel dizzy and sick with contained rage. Summoning her last bit of patience, Gia flashed Royce a demure smile, and chewed in silence.

The housekeeper brought in a serving tray.

"Oh goody!" Royce's green eyes smiled brightly. "The bacon has arrived!"

33

NOVEMBER 17TH

T hank God for pregnancy. Gia used the baby excuse to get away for a long break in the afternoon. Yes, she did feel queasy, that much was true—admittedly, she hadn't been able to keep lunch down.

Wanting to take her mind off present circumstances, she decided to ring Yiannis.

"*Koúklaki mou,*" his pleasant timbre carried her far away, "how are you? Where are you?"

"Ah, Yianni, I cannot begin to explain either of those things. Give me some news, please. How are things in Venice?"

"We are having a very strong month so far. Betting is up."

"Over last month or last year?"

"Both, actually."

"Fantastic. And Prince Kostas?"

She listened as Yiannis blew a heavy stream of air through his lips. "This is another matter entirely. He is not so easy to rehabilitate."

"Meaning?"

"He is very unhappy and does not listen to me. Always, he is late. Two times now I have caught him with one of those mafia peop—"

"Twice?" Gia interrupted. "Why did you not say anything?"

"Gia, my job is to do my job so that you can do yours."

"Thank you so much for that. I do want to know, though, what is going on with Kostas—always. If he is not better by the new year, I will take him to Greece. Are you reviewing the books from the other locations?"

"So far everything looks clean."

"Then Kostas is the only thief in our family?"

"You know that in every family there is always at least one thief, one gay, one lazy ass, one mamma's boy, and one prostitute."

She shook her head, "You almost have me laughing. You truly are the best, Cousin."

After hanging up with Yiannis, Gia phoned *La Nonna* for an update. She informed her of the sex tape and asked *La Nonna* to keep an eye on her sweaty mess of a cousin, Kostas. Gia suspected he was plotting something, or at least that his friends were.

Then she savored a few moments of silence, which were interrupted by the noisy arrival of Harper. After all the loud hellos that sounded from other parts of the house, Gia heard a door open on the floor below her. Gia cracked the door to the balcony and allowed Cameron and Harper's muffled voices to float up from the porch below.

"...found his doorman shot to death." Gia caught the end of what Harper had said.

"Honestly," Cam huffed, "you sound like you've been reading Reddit conspiracy theories."

"Not all conspiracies are fake news."

"Oh, sure."

"I think she did it."

"Had that guy in Spain shot?"

"All of it. The guy in Spain. Nico."

He snorted, "That is absurd."

"Is it? How do you know? You barely know her."

"First of all, Harper, that's bullshit. Gia has spent the last two months with me. I haven't seen a single thing that's off about her. The opposite, in fact! And I'm a very good judge of character. Second, when she isn't with me, she's working, so I don't even see when she would have the time to be the mastermind behind a string of international crimes."

"You really are naive sometimes, Big Brother. So what you're saying is that you don't find it remotely strange that she hid her relationship with Nico from you? Come on! We sat at Cipriani together in Venice, and Gia let me drone on about the murder case and never uttered a word! I think that's fucking psychopathic to be honest."

"No, Sis. You're just starting to eat up all that horseshit you shovel on TV."

"What are you even talking about?" Harper hissed, through gritted teeth.

"Not everyone's Ted Bundy for fuck's sake. Maybe Gia didn't say anything because she was worried you'd react exactly the way you're reacting. Just drop it, please."

Gia heard him stomp off. Harper's phone buzzed faintly, and she answered it in a whisper.

"You'll need more than that..." Gia strained her ears, but couldn't hear everything. She crouched and stuck her head ever so slightly out the door. " ...every room if you can. Did you try paying him? Right. It's a high-profile building, so that makes sense. Fine, so just the house in Venice then. Text me with the link when you're finished."

Realizing what she was hearing, Gia thought, *That little bitch is spying on me.*

Righting herself and shutting the door to the balcony, Gia grabbed her phone and texted *La Nonna*: *My boyfriend's sister is installing surveillance in Venice. Send a photographer.*

La Nonna responded quickly: *Why not return the favor? Install a few cameras at her house.*

* * *

GIA CHANGED into a caftan for dinner and braided her hair. Unlike the elaborate breakfast and lunch Cameron's parents had served, dinner was a simple affair. Bronwyn had dismissed the housekeeper and chef for the day and ordered Chinese takeout. Cameron escorted Gia into the library and the pair found cartons strewn around the coffee table, while Royce snapped unsuccessfully with some chopsticks at a pile of lo mein. Harper sat crossed-legged on the floor, picking at a plate of steamed broccoli.

"How was your nap, dear?" Bronwyn asked Gia. "Feeling rested?"

"Hi, Gia," Harper said, flashing a smile at Gia that was more like an animal showing its sharp teeth.

"Hello, Harper." Gia took a seat on the sofa next to Royce. Cam nestled in beside her. "Mrs. Langley, I do feel better, but no one told me that morning sickness lasts all day."

Harper dropped a broccoli floret on the floor. "You're... pregnant?"

Bronwyn interjected. "I wanted Cam-Cam and Gia to tell you."

"Wow." Harper sucked both her lips into her mouth and bit down hard, nodding down at her plate.

"Do you have anything to say to them?" Bronwyn asked, prodding Harper to mind her manners.

She didn't look up. "Hmm. Yeah. I have a lot of things to say. So many things."

"Harper," Royce said, chiding her like a teenager.

She eyed her brother and opened her mouth to speak but was unable to summon anything coherent.

"I think the word you're looking for is congratulations," Cameron growled.

"Let's go with that then." Harper tapped the coffee table with her chopsticks. "Gia, may I speak to you in private?"

"No," Cameron answered, "you may not."

Gia reached for his hand and squeezed it. "If that will make you feel at ease, Harper, I am glad to sp—"

"I agree with Cam-Cam," Royce said. "Now is not the time. Going forward we will be discussing all of these matters together. It's very important that we get everything on the table. We can't squabble. We need to be a unified front."

"You're absolutely right, darling," Bronwyn echoed. "Why don't you let the children know what you have in mind."

Royce faced Gia. "Sweetheart, we need to know... what's your level of involvement?"

Gia scrunched her face up, feigning innocence and confusion.

"Did you...uh... did you have that man killed?"

"Hint, Gia," Harper quipped sarcastically. "He's talking about Nico."

"Sorry," Gia shook her head, "you think I had something to do with all of this?"

"Perhaps..." Royce searched the ceiling for the words, "Nico hurt you? Maybe he was... abusive? Or... he was planning to sell the sex tape? Is there some... some motive... no, let's call it... excuse... as to why you might have felt you needed to do that? For example, maybe he threatened you in some way?"

Gia turned to Cameron looking for support and answers, but his eyes were closed, and his face was tight.

"I do not know what happened to Nico," Gia replied, turning her attention back to Royce. "We broke up weeks before."

"That's a lie," Harper jeered. "When I saw Nico's sister in Madrid, she told me that he was seeing someone in Venice but she wasn't sure who. And Jessica Joyce said... as I told you myself... that he was going to break up with someone in Venice in hopes of reconciling with her."

"Harper, I do not even believe I was in Venice then."

"Oh, yes you were. I have CCTV footage of you from that day."

"Then I must be confused. Forgive me, this is quite a shock, all of it. I am a very private person. I am not used to being in the spotlight like you, Harper."

"Is it true that you're laundering mafia money?" Harper tossed her head and narrowed her eyes at Gia.

"Stop it," Cameron was sizzling. He was definitely regretting coming to his parents.

But Harper stayed the course and would not be deterred. "Members of Cosa Nostra mafia have been seen in your... uh, establishments."

"We're getting off-topic," Royce clicked his tongue. "Let's imagine for a moment that everything that's bad is true—"

"It's not," Cameron insisted.

"But if it were," Royce continued, "then I think that's the place we should play from."

"I have no interest in participating in this," Harper said. "I'm not here to cover up for Gia."

"We're protecting your brother," Bronwyn explained.

"Like you *protected* Dad after you found out he jaunted off to Jeffrey Epstein's island?" Harper spat.

"That was for charity!" Royce defended himself, and then he seemed to get lost in his thoughts and faintly smirked. In that moment, Gia saw a bit of Harper in him. "Ironically... we were raising money to stop human trafficking."

"Sure, okay, Daddy."

"Enough, Harper!" Royce grabbed his soda and retreated to the back of the couch.

"Here is what we are going to do," Bronwyn said, leaning in. "Harper, you're going to bury that sex tape so no one ever sees it. Royce, you're going to have the boys deep fake a different camera angle from that security footage and make sure someone very different from Gia is on camera. Preferably Jessica Joyce. Maybe in a wig? Cameron, you're going to call work and take a sabbatical."

"Excuse me," Cam threw up his hand, "I don't think so. Bankers don't take sabbaticals."

"Cam, I will call Martin myself if I have to."

"You're going to call the owner of the bank to ask for vacation time for your son? Okay, Mom."

Bronwyn trained her eyes on her son, gazing lovingly. Then she cast her head down. "Darling, did you really think you got that job on your own?" She raised her eyes to meet Cameron's. He seemed very annoyed. "Honey... Martin will gladly let you have time to deal with family business. Trust me. He has to. And Gia, you will stay here with us until it's safe for you to go back to Europe. Lastly, Harper, my love, as soon as your Dad has the new footage ready, you're going on air with it."

"Am I, Mommy Dearest?"

"Jessica Joyce..." Bronwyn patted Royce on the knee.

"She's our Jane the Ripper," he responded, staring into his wife's oddly-tranquil eyes.

Bronwyn's home office, like the main estate, overlooked the Hudson River. The leaves were beginning to change, and the verdant valley was giving way to its annual bronzing. Once a carriage house, Bronwyn had renovated the stone structure to her liking, and created a large, comfortable sitting area with multiple TV screens—it was her own cozy newsroom. Upstairs was a conference room table that sat up to twenty.

Truth be told, Bronwyn rarely went into the city anymore, and she had everything she needed right here; she detested midtown and the ugly, foreboding OTN complex, filled to the brim with ass-grabbing old boys and giggling blondes wearing miles of hair extensions and bedecked in fluttering, false eyelashes.

The housekeeper, a German lady, brought a tea tray in and laid it on the coffee table in front of where Bronwyn and Gia sat. The latter thanked the woman.

"I had Anna make biscotti for you," Bronwyn said, taking a sip of black tea without sugar.

"How kind, thank you."

"Cam is quite taken with you, Gia." Bronwyn smiled. "We've never seen him this happy, honestly. He is very protective of you."

Gia felt her heart twist in a sweet way. Love maybe? It was strange for her feelings to oscillate in this way, from suffocation to satisfaction.

"He is extraordinary, your son."

"We like to think so." Bronwyn wrinkled her nose, and her eyes twinkled. "I have two little gifts for you." She tiptoed over to the kitchenette and retrieved one box and one bag from a cabinet. "Open this one first."

She handed Gia a black box with a black ribbon. Gia untied the bow and lifted the lid. Inside was a pregnancy test kit from the pharmacy.

"I would like for you to take this test. Now, please." Her eyes were still shining, but her expression was detached and cold and very out of place, divorced from the reality of how inappropriate her request was. "The bathroom is behind the wall with the fireplace."

Gia held the kit in her lap. "You do not trust me."

"I don't even know you, dear."

Right. Bronwyn sipped her tea, her legs politely crossed at the ankles—you have to do such things to avoid varicose veins. One thing was sure, Cameron got his comfort with silence from this woman. From her armchair, Bronwyn silently projected nothing but complete confidence.

"I see." Gia took the test and stood. "*Bene...*"

Sighing deeply, she strolled to the bathroom and did what was asked of her. After twelve minutes she reemerged. Bronwyn's cloudy blue eyes were fixed, watching her network, sound muted, closely reading the captions.

Gia extended the plastic stick toward her, and Bronwyn plucked a tissue from a ceramic holder, wrapping it around the testing stick before accepting it. Bronwyn studied the little screen for a moment— a pink plus sign. Suddenly she felt irritated that Royce had not bought more tests, of different varieties, like the one with the smiley face, or the one that spells it out for you in words—pregnant or not pregnant. She would have asked Gia to take an entire shelf full of the tests if it made a difference. But it didn't. Cam had made his choice, and now a little Cam-Cam was on the way.

"Congratulations," Bronwyn said, passing Gia the second gift. It was an iconic light blue bag, Tiffany. Surely whatever was inside this one must be more benign. Gia unwrapped layers of tissue paper to reveal a sterling silver baby rattle. She took it out and shook it comically. This made Bronwyn laugh. Engraved on the rattle: *Welcome to the family.*

"Gia, dear, I would appreciate it very much if you keep the first gift between just the two of us. Do you understand?"

At the tip-top of Bronwyn's high pitched voice, there was a nearly imperceptible layer of thin ice. Gia understood Cameron's mother very well indeed. This new request of hers was simply another test.

35

Marina unwrapped the carved wooden figurines of the nativity as Francesca handed them to her. The decoration had been passed down to Francesca from her grandparents. It was her grandfather who had whittled the scene and the figurines, and her grandmother who painted the pieces. Some of the animals were missing tails or ears, but the little baby Jesus, wrapped in his cotton diaper, was still in good condition and extra chubby.

Luca came into the house carrying several kinds of fish, which he placed in the sink and covered with a bit of ice. After he washed his hands, he walked to Marina and placed them on her shoulders. He bent over and kissed her under her ear. Marina put her palm over her belly and imagined what it would feel like to stroke her growing baby's head—only a week until her due date. She leaned back and puckered her lips at Luca, and he happily obliged her.

Vittore let the door slam as he burst into Francesca's house. "*Amici!* I bring wonderful news. We have located a buyer!"

Having spent the better part of the last year working with an unscrupulous lawyer, Vittore had sent their chests of gold to buyers around the globe. Splitting up the money into batches was part of the plan. Some of the deals had been cash and others were trades. The lawyer helped them funnel the money into numerous currency-generating businesses. Marina and Luca now owned several casinos throughout Europe—not that they had the faintest idea how to run them. It was all a grand experiment.

"Vittore," Marina said, "I want you to take the money from this deal." She had made great strides in learning Italian while living with Luca and Francesca.

Vittore took her hand, "I would never dream of doing that, *Sirena*. No, all I want is enough money to buy the barbershop. That... and the love of my friends... is everything I need."

"You, Vittore Cantalupi, are an angel from heaven," Francesca beamed and came over just to ruffle his hair.

Luca looked around the room and wondered how he got so lucky. He had a beautiful woman to cherish, the joy of his first child on the way, and a great fortune. Life was beautiful.

"Breaking news," Harper read from the teleprompter. "OTN has received an alternate angle of the surveillance footage of Nicolás Ángel Fernández and a female companion in the lobby of his Madrid apartment building. We can confirm that this woman is Jessica Joyce. Ms. Joyce previously stated that she had not seen Nico in months; however, this explosive new tape places her with him just days before his disappearance at the Venice Film Festival."

Royce dipped his hand into a bowl of popcorn and emitted a pleasured, "Mmm!" Between crunches, he spoke, "Mmm! Yes, this is great. Harper is so good." His daughter's face peered back at them from one of the large TV screens in Bronwyn's office. All of the other screens, tuned into competitive news channels, were muted. The other channels were droning on about the same news that they had for weeks: the election debacle.

The producers of Harper's show cut to the freshly edited footage —which of course was completely fake. A few seconds was all it took. Even though it was grainy, the footage was spectacularly constructed; there she was, Jessica Joyce in disguise, holding Nico's hand. The tape played over and over on a loop.

While Bronwyn had only requested one deep fake, Royce and his boys upped the ante and altered the existing footage to make Gia's profile resemble that of Jessica Joyce. The result was uncanny. Gia could hardly believe she was looking at a film that had been doctored. Per Royce's instruction, the Langley's investigator had leaked both clips far and wide half an hour before Harper went live with the news. And earlier that day, the investigator had reached out to his contact in Russia to put his troll farms on the case. So, in less time than it takes to boot up a PC, those clips were seeded across the Surface Web, Deep Web, and Dark Web. Scattered to the wind, they took root in the hearts and minds of the masses of easily influenced sheeple, and what bloomed was a veritable forest of conspiracy theories.

"Impressive, huh, Cam-Cam?" Royce raised his eyebrows many times in a row.

Cam didn't respond. Instead, he eyeballed Gia, who spoke, because she could tell that Royce was quite proud of himself, and felt it would be rude not to praise him. "How did you do this?" she inquired.

Royce chuckled, "The fruit of years in the edit bay, Gia. Years!" He playfully slapped Bronwyn's thigh. "Right, dear? Remember the early days when we had to fumble with the negative cutter and all that mess?"

Bronwyn giggled, which sounded very odd, like muffled screams from someone locked in a basement.

"Technology," Bronwyn marveled.

She and Royce locked eyes and shared a deep sigh. Bronwyn had always wanted to be at the top of the food chain, and when she and Royce came together in a crisis, she knew they were unstoppable. She felt a rush of sexual energy for her husband, and when it flashed across her eyes, it was clear that he could feel it, too. One thing was certain: Royce Langley was getting lucky tonight.

Although only a few feet separated Gia and Cameron, she felt worlds apart from him. Yesterday, when Bronwyn insisted on monopolizing Gia over the course of the afternoon, Harper had taken

Cameron into town. He'd been cool and withdrawn since then. Gia wondered what poison had dripped from Harper's lips into Cam's ears.

Truthfully, when he pulled away, Gia felt more invested, not that she let him in on that line of thinking. To Cameron, Gia seemed more aloof than ever. After exiting the shower that morning, a strange thought had occurred to him for the first time: *Maybe she'll lose the baby.*

Just ten days ago they'd floated on the Mediterranean, and he'd shouted about falling in love, but now Gia had landed him in a nightmare.

"Everything all right, darling?" Bronwyn asked her son.

"This is a dream come true, Mom," Cameron said, flatly. "Watching you and Dad manipulate America like two sociopaths is a real blast."

Immediately, the temperature changed in the room.

"Apologize to your mother right now!" Royce screamed, slamming his popcorn down on the side table. The last few kernels jingled against the glass bowl.

Cameron snorted and muttered under his breath. Then he rose and charged out of Bronwyn's office. It did not go unnoticed by Gia that his family made him act like an entitled child.

At that moment, Gia forced herself to cry. She covered her face and hiccupped little sobs. Inside she actually felt like screaming and hurling Royce's popcorn bowl at Harper's face, either on TV or in person.

Bronwyn slid over to Gia and rubbed her hands on Gia's back. "Go after him," Bronwyn whispered.

Leading a performance that included fat tears and light whimpers, Gia said, "Thank you both. I do not know what happened to Nico, but I am in over my head."

I am not. Am I? she wondered, feeling a growing sense of anxiety.

Leaving the room, Gia took her sweet time finding Cameron. She strayed off of the estate's lit pathways and ambled through the darkness. What she wouldn't give to drag the lot of them to the bottom of the Hudson. The gills in her arms ruffled in a way that hurt. Eventually, she found Cameron huddled under a heat lamp in a gazebo. She lingered on the steps.

"I don't know if I can do this," Cam said, staring into the night sky.

"No one said you have to."

"Gia, tell me that everything is going to go back to the way it was before."

She didn't respond.

He shuffled around in a circle. "When did you see him last?"

Gia tossed her hands up like she did not know what he was talking about.

"Harper told me that another one of your boyfriends died."

"What?"

"Pierre," Cameron answered simply.

Feeling suddenly woozy, Gia sat down on the steps. She hadn't heard that name in forever. Cameron began knocking his knuckles against the wood railing, waiting for an answer.

"That was fifteen years ago."

"Really? Did you have someone cut his throat, too?"

"Is this what you think, seriously?" She let out a breathy gasp, but it sounded like a laugh. Maybe it was a laugh because she found this conversation ridiculous. "Pierre killed himself. And he broke my fucking heart when he did that."

"Is that what's wrong with you?"

"Excuse me?"

"Never mind." He was rapping his fist harder against the wood. "I don't know what to think... what to believe. I... I hate this shit!" He slammed his hand down hard.

"What is it you want to hear, Cameron?"

"How about I love you?"

"I love you."

"Do you mean that?"

"*Amore*, I am pregnant with your child. If I did not love you, would I keep this baby? Would I be here, defending myself against your parents and your sister? Do you not understand that sometimes the way love speaks is through what you do, the actions you take, and not what you whisper after making love?"

"Hmm." He nodded to himself and spoke softly under his breath. "She loves me."

"She does."

He rushed over to her and wrapped her in his arms, kissing her hard. "Say it again."

"I love you."

He unbuckled his pants. "Touch me." He brought her hand between his legs. "Goddamn you, Gia. Do you see how hard you make me?" He bit her bottom lip and held his hand on top of hers while she stroked him. "I would make you pregnant again if I could." He tugged a handful of her hair and she arched back. "Say it again."

"I love you."

He brought her head down to him, and she took him in her mouth. He thrust himself inside of her while he held the back of her neck.

"You're mine, Gia."

He moved his hips harder against her. His breath was shaky.

"Take it. Deeper."

She opened her mouth wider, and let him sink into her throat. She slid her hands around him, caressed him, and then pulled him into her. He came, and she swallowed everything he gave her. As he was going soft, Cameron dropped down onto the floor between Gia's legs.

"You've got me on my knees, Gia. Don't hurt me."

37

JULY 1985

From beneath a wide straw hat that featured a bright turquoise band, Marina watched her daughter eat an omelet. Gia was becoming such a beautiful young girl; at fifteen she shared the same heart-shaped face as Luca, and her eyes sparkled with the freshness and wonder of youth. On the terrace of the Hôtel Hermitage, the prideful Monte Carlo sun shone its finest morning glow.

"Be careful on the boat with Papa today, *koúklaki mou*."

Gia smiled at her mamma and nodded. After Gia left to meet her father at the dock, Marina relaxed into a chair by the pool, enjoying a rare moment alone. She shimmied out of her blue caftan and popped on a pair of large sunglasses. Her enormous diamond studs cast crystalline rainbows on her navy maillot, and she twisted her light red hair into a knot. Ordering a Kir Royale, she signed the bill to her room, which happened to be the biggest suite at the resort. After half an hour or so, she got too warm and dipped into the pool.

Treading water in the deep end was a man with olive skin and a grim aura. Marina felt shock flood her body as she realized that she knew that face, though it had been many years since she'd seen it: Adonis.

She was bound to run into him at some point, and that thought helped her control her emotions at his appearance. After all, the higher you go in life, the less oxygen there is, and few survive at the top. Marina and Adonis were both wealthy, and Monaco had always lured the rich and famous.

It was evident that he recognized her, too, and his eyes were wide with disbelief; he'd all but stopped paddling under the water because his limbs had gone numb. Adonis had barely thought of her since that dark night, and he had been successful in putting her out of his mind.

He'd convinced himself—and his friends—that disposing of her had been as necessary as taking out the trash on garbage day. It was an unpleasant and unfortunate event, and now, seeing her in the shallow water, he suddenly felt horror, regret even, at what he'd done when he was young. He did not take his eyes off of her as she exited the pool, picked up her things, and disappeared into the hotel.

My God, how much she's changed, he pondered. She was a real woman now with curves and a more mature, elegant presence than when he knew her. He thought of chasing after her, but to what end?

Adonis lingered on the steps of the pool with a heaviness that was full of curiosity. As he flashed to that summer so long ago, he felt odd nostalgia and his mind replaced his version of Marina with this one. His memories were no longer ugly. This spotting had transfigured the past into something sweet and romantic. Remembering their adventure, he thought of exploring the Cyclades with her, seeking the treasure he never found.

A sense of excitement and possibility swept over him, and he wished he could go back in time with this Marina and change everything. The intervening years had their ups and downs, and particularly after his first divorce and the second and third, after nearly all of his children curdled on him, he felt lonely but never stopped his search for loose women—or marriageable ones with morals that aligned with his.

Adonis pulled himself from the pool and dried off. He entered the hotel and stopped by the front desk, with an impulse to inquire after her. Stunned, he felt his spirits soar when he discovered that she left a note for him.

Meet me in room 511.

All at once he was in college again, but now he was James Bond— Sean Connery's interpretation—and he felt so alive. He scurried up to his room, showered lickety-split, and splashed on more cologne than necessary.

What was he even thinking?

He paused and inspected his reflection in the bathroom mirror. He'd earned a Greek belly, but he was not too bad-looking. Maybe closure would be good, maybe she had forgiven him years ago, and he so longed to know... well, how she survived? What circumstances had lifted that little village girl from Santorini and landed her smack in the upper echelon of European society? He was determined to know. He tipped on a white Panama hat and pressed the elevator button.

Adonis rapped anxiously on the door to 511, a small suite. Marina was on the other side of the doorframe, wearing a light blue, button-up mini dress and espadrilles. She waved him in without a word and took a seat at a table near the sliding door to the terrace.

He stood above her, taking her in, peeking down her dress to catch a glimpse of her bra, and when he did, he felt very aroused. Clearing his throat, he sat down across from her, crossing his leg to hide his erection.

"I may need a drink for this," she said.

"Okay, yes. Sure."

She got up and bent over to reach in the minibar, and when she did, he saw a flash of her lace panties, and he had the urge to unzip his pants and take her right there. However, he'd long since learned to temper that kind of behavior, since it had become ever so much more difficult to do as you pleased with a woman, after the Lib movement and all that. He wasn't sure he could risk it. After all, he didn't know anything about her, and what if she complained to someone? A scandal would not be good for business. He wasn't in the mood to grease palms and shut down rumblings about him at this point in time. So he just sat there, with his lap starting to throb. He did not remember having wanted her so badly back when they were kids, but perhaps he had.

She dropped two cubes of ice in a crystal tumbler and gave it to him, along with a little bottle of vodka. He drained it into the glass, and took a sip, resting his tongue on the smooth edge of the cup. Marina took nervous sips directly from her bottle.

She scrunched her face into a mess of lines. "I do not want to talk about what happened that night."

"Really?" Adonis was shocked. The whole day felt off-kilter, really.

Marina handed them two more bottles. Gin this time.

"Drink," she said, sternly, and he swallowed. "More."

"Where have you been all this time?"

She served him another bottle of clear spirits. "France."

"Wow. Did you... did you marry, have kids?"

"No. Drink."

He was feeling quite giddy now. She wasn't married. Interesting. He thirsted for a scotch, but there was none.

Marina stood by the glass door and stared out at the sea, thinking of Luca. "Did you ever find your shipwreck?" As she spoke, she did not turn around to look at Adonis.

"Eventually." He could almost laugh. "It was just a hunk of rotting wood. Treasure... what a joke."

"Get on the bed."

Adonis nearly spit out his drink. "Come again?"

"The bed."

Robotically, he carried himself over to the end of the bed as she had commanded.

She stormed over to him and slapped him hard across his bearded cheek. He swayed and then shook his face. Fair enough. He probably deserved that.

"Take your clothes off and lay down," she said, through gritted teeth.

He did as she asked, very gladly.

Marina reached under the pillow and pulled out a soft, terry cloth belt. She tied his hands to one side of the bed frame.

Glaring at him, she hissed, "You left me to die, you vulgar piece of shit."

It was the truth. What could he say? He did not feel ashamed; in fact, he was aroused again. It was rather fun not to be in control sometimes.

"Close your eyes." Her voice was a growl.

He heard her feet crush against the carpet and then the clinking of ice in the bucket. She sat next to him on the bed, grabbed a handful of ice, and cupped his balls.

"Ahhhh!" He screamed.

"Shut the fuck up and close your eyes."

Marina threw the ice on the carpet. He laid there, eyes closed, waiting to feel her knees on either side of him, hoping she would push those white panties to the side and take him inside her. His chest pounded at the thought. The last thing he heard was the sound of sloshing water and popping ice as Marina struck his head with all the fury she had in her.

Adonis awoke sometime later—how much later he did not know —but his head ached something awful, both from the blow and from the booze. He blinked his eyes, trying to clear his vision. His arms had fallen asleep, and they stung now. He wriggled his body as best as he could to wake them up. Fortunately, she had not used her sailing knots on him.

"Aghh," he groaned deeply as he let himself loose. Sitting there for a moment, trying to make sense of everything, Adonis suddenly noticed something on the bedside table.

It was a gold coin—irregularly shaped and green with age. Picking it up, he took note that it was thick and weighty, the shape of a messy wax seal. Also on the table was a note in Marina's handwriting: *Ade gamísou.* Fuck off.

Turning the coin over and over in his palm, he held it up to one eye. He'd seen coins like this in trading magazines in college—they had been the reason why he had been inspired to fly to Greece in the summer of '69, much to his father's dismay.

In that moment, Adonis's brain was groggy, but he wasn't stupid. He had put it all together.

That bitch had found the gold.

The money was his, and she had stolen it from him. Marina never intended to get closure today. She wasn't trying to revenge-fuck him; she had already fucked him years ago. He should have squeezed her skinny little neck and cracked it when he had the chance.

He threw on his clothes and winced in pain as his hat passed over the bump on his head. Heading straight to the lobby, he did his best to contain his anger and strolled up to the check-in girl.

"Hi there," he flashed her a smile. "I ran into my friend from college by the pool... her name is Marina Galanis. I would love to... to take her to dinner and catch up. Could you tell me her room number?"

"Galanis?" The girl frowned. "Mmm."

"She's really beautiful, strawberry hair, pretty blue eyes... like yours."

She smiled at him. "Oh! Marina Acquaviva. She just checked out of the *Diamond Suite*." She lowered her voice when offering up the name of the room because she really wasn't supposed to give out guest information.

He sucked his teeth. "That is very, very disappointing. Could I leave her a message perhaps?"

"The bellhop already took her bags down to the dock." She leaned in close to him. "If you run, maybe you can catch her. Her boat is called 'The Adonis'."

Rage howled inside him so powerfully that he felt he might combust. His whole body tensed, and he forced a smile. "Thank you very much."

With that, he began a controlled fast-walk. He needed to move quickly, but he didn't want to bring attention to himself by running. On the far side of the pool, he passed the bellhop, who was returning with an empty cart.

In the distance, he spied Marina as she kissed a man with curly black hair. The tension in his body could have made his eyes bleed. As he approached the top of the dock, he heard the engine start. Marina was engaged in conversation with the man and a teenage girl. There was a loud mechanical clanking as they pulled up the anchor, and Adonis moved faster. The boat pushed off slowly, but he ran furiously to the end of the dock finally jumping and clearing the gap between the dock and the stern. When he landed, Gia saw him and screamed.

Luca was at the wheel, and by the time Marina spotted Adonis, he was already very close to her.

"Mamma!" Gia screeched.

"Keep driving!" Marina yelled at Luca.

But everything happened too fast, within seconds maybe. Adonis put his hands around Marina as he had done sixteen years ago and wrang her neck with all his might, watching her face go red. But this time, in Marina's arms, her sharp gills emerged, like the flap of a jet's wing, and she used the last of her power to slice clean across his throat. His blood exploded onto her, and they fell together, his weight crashing her head hard against the wall of the boat.

They were in a limp heap before Gia or Luca could do anything about it. Her mother's head was bleeding, as was this horrible man's neck, and their blood spread across the deck, so much so that it was impossible to tell whose blood was whose. Gia doubled over and shrieked with an otherworldly pain.

"Mamma!" Gia picked up her mother's head, cradling it, but it was lifeless and strangely light. It bent from her neck in an unnatural way, and Gia cried out and dropped it, where it landed with a thud on the wood. Gia felt horrible, because what if she had hurt her mother even more?

"Mamma, please! Mamma! Wake up, please!"

Luca couldn't think. He only drove, far enough into the sea that no other boats were around. Gia threw herself into his lap and sobbed without stopping. Once they dropped anchor, Luca held Gia in his arms and screamed and cried out of grief. They stayed like that for so long that the sun set. When the tears finally stopped and their chests were empty of breath and heavy with sorrow, they looked down at the floor. Gia screamed again and shook uncontrollably, burying her head in her father's neck.

Mamma, Mamma, Mamma. I know she will wake up. I know she will.

It wasn't possible that Marina could be gone for good. And Luca also thought his wife might come back to life, just as she had on the deck of the boat when he pulled her from the sea many years ago.

Of course, they couldn't go to the police. How could they? And Luca knew this man to be Adonis—while older, Luca recognized him from the time when he first saw him.

Luca was so angry, so angry, so angry. Gia was shaking in his arms and he stroked her hair. He had to find it in himself to be strong for her, and he had to figure out a plan. He held Gia until she fell into an uneasy sleep, and he put her down on the seat in the back of the boat like a small child.

The only thing that came to mind was Vittore, and after Vittore, Venice. He and Gia would need to take the bodies to Venice. He washed the blood off the deck before it dried. His heart ached and he wondered if the pain would make his chest explode. He trembled as he wiped the blood from Marina's face, noting that her hair was soaked with it and drying quickly.

He covered the bodies with a tarp. The next morning he dragged them down into the belly of the boat. Gia stared at him as he did this, rocking back and forth. He brought blankets and pillows and food from downstairs, and they sealed the door to the cabin.

Sailing the distance from Monte Carlo to Venice, stopping only for gas along the way, Gia was numb from the trauma. Her brain looped and looped around, trying to make sense of what she'd seen. She had nightmares that the man rose from the dead and tried to kill her.

Once they arrived in Venice, Luca had no choice, he sent Gia swimming in the canals, looking for a place to hide the bodies. She found one, an underwater cave beneath the Hotel Bauman. There were pilings down there and rocks and she had to make several trips back to her father out on the lagoon in the middle of the night. First for a chain, which was so heavy that she almost dropped it a few times. But her tail gave her the strength to swim, and she was able to get the chains into the deep.

Then, she returned to the boat for her mother's body.

The smell was awful. She threw up in the water as her father pushed her mother into the lagoon, head first, followed by her silvery-blue tail. After that, it was the man's turn. He was red and bloated, and his body produced horrible, disgusting grumbles. She tried to ignore the fact that he seemed to be leaking.

But down he went, too, under Venice, to rot.

Unfortunately, Gia only had one chain and she loathed the idea of wrapping her mother together with that monstrous stranger, sealing them to a piling with the chain and a padlock for eternity.

Her stomach turned and flopped as she swam away, sick at leaving her mother in this watery grave.

"I will come back, Mamma, I promise. I promise I will."

38

NOVEMBER 26TH

Gia's phone rang early in the morning, waking her up abruptly. She slipped out of bed, careful not to disturb Cam, and onto the balcony. It was Yiannis.

"Is something wrong?" she whispered into the phone.

"Kostas is missing," replied Yiannis. "He did not come to work yesterday. Of course, I thought he was just being a lazy bastard, so I did not worry too much about it... but after he did not show up this morning, I checked his apartment, and he was not there. His suitcase was missing and most of his clothes."

Gia sighed, feeling frustrated once again with her cousin. "I will take care of this, do not worry."

"There is something else, *koúkla mou*. I am very sorry to tell you this."

"Spit it out, Yianni, what?" she snapped.

"He has taken money from the safe."

"How much?"

"More than a hundred thousand."

"*Why* did he have the code, Yianni? You *know* he is not trustworthy."

"Of course, of course. I would never give him the code. We do not know how he got in, and if his plan was to steal, why would he not take everything?"

"Because he knew I would kill him if he did," Gia responded. "I will call you back later, Yianni. Carry on with the day as normal."

She slinked back inside, but Cameron was awake. "Who was that?" he asked, concern in his voice. "You sounded upset."

"Casino business. Everything is fine." She pulled her silk night-gown over her head so that she was standing in the room wearing only her panties. Reaching for the sheet, she tugged it off little by little, leaving Cameron exposed in his boxers. Over the course of the past week, she had made love to him every chance she got. Sex kept him happy and, more importantly, it shut him up.

Afterward, while Cameron showered, Gia dialed Italy.

"Congratulations, *angioletta*," *La Nonna* said on the other end of the line. "Those Americans know what they are doing."

Since debuting the Jane the Ripper narrative starring Jessica Joyce, Harper and OTN had managed to make their version of the facts in Nico's murder investigation the only plausible explanation. All the major news outlets, and therefore the public, accepted that the original footage wasn't the best angle at which to view Nico and his female companion. The closer footage—the deep fake—that was the money shot. And it was the only clip news channels even played anymore.

"They even managed to make her look guilty!" *La Nonna* cackled, erupting into her predictable pattern of laughter, annoying Gia.

"*Ascolta, vecchia—*"

"No need to be rude Gia! I am already listening. I am your humble servant."

"My cousin Kostas has stolen money from the casino in Venice and has gone missing. I need you to find him."

"I will send my crew today."

"Hold onto him. I have to deliver him to my grandparents, so I want him in good shape."

"Understood."

Gia hid the burner phone before Cameron emerged from the bathroom.

"What would you like to do this morning, baby?" he asked her. It wasn't even six o'clock in the morning, so Royce and Bronwyn would be sleeping for at least another hour. "What if we take the boat out?"

"No fishing," she wrinkled her nose.

"Too bad." He tapped his finger on the end of her nose. "We're up before the sun, so we'd have the best catch."

"I already have the best catch."

"Look at that grin! Miss Acquaviva, you are giving yourself away." She swatted him on the arm, and he picked her up and tossed her on the bed. "Tell me what you want to do, or I'm going to be forced to fuck you again!"

"I can be persuaded..."

"Woman, you'll be the death of me!" She crawled her fingers up his chest and wrapped her hands around his neck, pretending to choke him. He wrestled her and flipped her over and gave her three slaps on her ass before hopping out of bed. "Meet me at the car in fifteen. I'll make us some toast."

The car! The prospect of leaving the Langley estate for the first time in ten days was thrilling. Gia showered and dressed in a whirlwind.

Cameron met her by the Mercedes SUV with what was apparently her breakfast.

"What is this?" she asked, critically examining a sad piece of white bread covered by a slice of American cheese.

"Cheese toast!"

"If you call this breakfast, then I think I understand why Americans have such a high rate of heart attacks," she chided.

"Come on! I used to make this as my breakfast every morning before school when my parents were at work."

"Oh, *amore*, how sad."

"It's the breakfast of champions!" he insisted, cranking the engine. "I have a surprise for you."

They zipped along the dark country roads for a while and crossed a bridge over the Hudson. A few moments later, Cameron pulled off the road and drove to the top of a gravel parking lot, where a security guard met them.

"It's all yours, folks," the guard said, ushering them into her heated golf cart. Cameron winked at her and took the wheel.

"I called my buddy to open this place up for us." He beamed as he zoomed along the trails in what Gia considered nothing more than a souped-up lawnmower. They passed enormous sculptures in open fields of grass. Finally, he stopped at the edge of a hill and bolted from the golf cart. "Hurry! I don't want to miss it!" Jogging to an elevator, Gia followed and they were lifted onto a platform that overlooked the rolling landscape in front of them. Together, they watched as the sun broke over the hills.

"Happy Thanksgiving, baby," Cameron said, pulling Gia in for a hug.

She sighed. "My first ever." This made Cameron crack a huge smile, thinking that he loved being her "first" anything.

The rest of the morning, the pair spent exploring Storm King, and Cameron chatted easily about all of his favorite installations. She shared his enthusiasm for art and made a mental note to take him for a private visit to the Peggy Guggenheim next time he was in Venice. As they observed their warped reflections in Anish Kapoor's Light & Landscape, Gia said, "I think Jeff Koons borrows a lot of ideas from Anish."

"All artists steal from other artists, Gia."

"Is that what Jeff told you?" she scoffed. He blew a raspberry at her. She shoved him a little. "I knew it!"

One corner of his mouth turned up. "I love us like this. All the craziness aside... honestly, I always saw myself like this... sharing the things I love with the one I love. I feel like I've been waiting for someone like you for so long. I've been on my own a lot, and it's not what I want anymore. I want to be with you, Gia."

Before she could respond, his phone rang.

"Harpie," he said as he answered, "are you at Mom and Dad's already? Oh, shit, I didn't realize that... sure, yeah, we'll head there now." He slipped his cell back in his pocket as his smile sagged. "Time to go." He escorted her to the car by her hand, and while he was driving, Gia rested her hand on his thigh.

Inside, Gia felt a blade of emotions sawing at her. On one end was her strong desire for independence, the runway to be as bad as she would like. On the other was the temping warmth of Cameron and his promises for love and a family all her own. Both ends of the spectrum were wonderful and appealing, but everything in the middle cut her in half with a thousand sharp teeth.

When they arrived at the house, the smells of the pending feast greeted them at the door.

"Just in time!" Harper said, swinging the front door wide open. "Cam-Cam, it's time for our tradition."

"My favorite part of the day!" He ran behind Harper into the kitchen. "You grab the pie, I'll scoop the ice cream."

Gia sauntered in behind them, watching them scramble around. Harper stole a pumpkin pie out of the oven, and Cameron took a vat of freshly-made ice cream from the walk-in freezer.

"Hello, lover," Harper whispered to the pie. She sliced a piece out and let it plop onto her mother's bone china.

"MEXICAN VANILLA, HARPIE!" Cameron whisper-screamed to his sister, as two big balls of ice cream fell onto the plate beside the pie.

"I could cry," Harper said, eyeing the pie. "In fact, I think I might. Fork!"

Cameron kicked his knees high as he danced his way over to the silverware and back. Gia, standing to the side of the kitchen, watched in quiet fascination as the seemingly adolescent scene played out in front of her.

"Kids?" Bronwyn called them from somewhere far away.

"Hurry up!" Cameron said, distributing three forks. "Eat before they get in here."

Harper dug in and with a full mouth mumbled, "I'm definitely going to cry. I haven't had dessert since last year. Fuck TV. Oh. My. Godddddddd."

Cam laughed, and a small stream of ice cream leaked onto his chin.

The kitchen door opened with a thud, and Bronwyn stood there mouth agape.

"Not again! Give me that pie right now."

Cameron and Gia giggled, and he put an oven mitt on, picked up the pie, and made a run for it.

"You can have it if you can catch me!"

"Cameron Charles Langley! If you drop my pumpkin pie, I swear I will ship you on a slow boat back to London! Put down the pie!"

He lapped a few times around the kitchen for dramatic effect.

"Honestly, I don't understand the two of you," Bronwyn stole back her beloved pumpkin pie and placed in it a safe location. "I think next year I might just have the pie delivered at the end of the meal and put a stop to this wretched tradition. It just ruins the look of the table when the centerpiece... the *pie*... has been all nibbled."

Cameron and Harper exchanged conspiratorial glances and snickered silently.

They are very lucky, Gia thought. *They have each other.*

She stifled a pang in her heart. The truth was when Cameron was around his family, she felt superfluous. To him, he believed as though she fit right in, like she'd always been there. The experience for Gia was very much like a long rack focus; the more Cameron and his family talked, the more she faded into the background. Sometimes when they droned on and on and gesticulated in their distinctly animated ways, she could feel herself merging with the sofa or melting into the floor. Being with Cameron was one thing; she could handle that. However, she did love walking away to be at her own apartment. But being with his family? It was exhausting having to be "on" all the time.

They gathered around the dining table just after lunchtime, so that they could eat as a family before the driver took Harper and Royce into the city. Even the holidays couldn't keep Harper from her prime nine o'clock time slot.

Bronwyn laid out the Thanksgiving table herself—the epitome of

Martha Stewart chic. Featuring a runner of small pastel gourds and tapered candles of different heights, the pale colors made Bronwyn's light green china the star of the setting.

Suddenly, Royce powered up the electric carver as if it were a chainsaw and held it in the air, "Let's get this show on the road!"

"Before we start," Harper stood up with her champagne flute in her hand, "I'd like to make a toast."

"What a lovely idea, sweetheart," Bronwyn said, head high. "I'm all for it."

Harper raised her glass to Gia. "To Gia Acquaviva... I never thought my brother would settle down, so you have worked your magic on him. I'm finding out something new about you every day." Harper glanced down at the table and picked up her knife, holding its edge against the rim of the crystal. She took a deep breath before she continued, "I know you killed Nico you fucking bitch, and if you so much as touch my brother in a way I don't like, I will slice your fucking throat myself." With that, she swung her knife so hard that her glass broke.

"Jesus Christ, Harper!" Cameron screamed.

Gia admired Harper's guts, she really did. Keeping her cool, she pushed her chair back and rose to face Harper, eye-to-eye, across the table.

"I believe I am intruding on your family time," Gia said, words falling silky smooth from her lips. "How rude of me." She turned her attention to Bronwyn. "Mrs. Langley, thank you very much for this beautiful meal and for your hospitality. However, it is time for me to go home."

Gia strode away from the table with an easy grace, like she was walking to the shops on a Sunday afternoon. With each step she took, the world fell away. Behind her, all sounds blended together—like Cameron and Harper yelling at each other and the swishing of Bronwyn sweeping up broken glass.

This is better. This is right, Gia thought. *I am intruding.*

She knew she didn't belong in a Norman Rockwell painting. She picked up her phone and rang the jet captain to ready her plane. She asked him to call a car to pick her up as well.

Cameron galloped after her, trying to talk to her as she was packing, working his hardest to convince her to stay. But Gia felt like everything had slowed down. He seemed muffled and she couldn't understand what he was saying, so she just kept packing. He put his hand on the suitcase, but she moved it off.

The captain texted that the car would be there in ten minutes. She realized for the first time that she was hungry and felt light-headed.

No matter, she'd eat on the jet.

It felt like there was a layer of vaseline covering everything outside of her immediate personal space. When she was finished with her suitcase, she zipped it tight and jerked it upright.

Cameron blocked the door. She took several breaths and then tried to walk out, hoping he would just move to the side. He didn't.

"Don't go, Gia."

"Please move."

"No, I want you to stay with me."

"Cameron, I want to leave."

"Then just wait and I'll pack and go with you."

"No. I want to go alone."

His hands dropped off the doorframe and to his sides. "You don't mean that. You're just upset. Look, I told Harper she can't say those kinds of disrespectful things to you."

"This is not for me." Gia looked at the ceiling.

"What are you talking about?"

"I am not a family-oriented person, Cameron. You should find yourself a nice girl and get married."

He was so stunned that he couldn't even think of what to say.

"And as for the baby, I am still in the first trimester. I will schedule an abortion for next week."

Cameron absolutely crumbled. His body lost the ability to stand upright, and he doubled over and stumbled his way into the guest room, landing on the edge of the bed.

Gia made her way through the open door and carried her suitcase down the stairs. Rolling the bag along the grey plank floors of the foyer and past the noisy pavers in the Langley's driveway, she didn't stop walking until she passed the iron gate at the entrance to the estate. She never looked back, not even once.

39

G ia opened her eyes. Sixteen didn't feel any different than fifteen to her. This day, her birthday, was as horrible as all of the other days had been since summer. In fact, this day was worse, since her mother was not alive to wake her with a song and a gold coin, as she had done every year since Gia was born.

The palazzo was empty and dank, so Gia set a fire in the hearth. On the mantle was her grandmother's nativity set. She picked up a wooden donkey and stroked it in her palm. Checking in on her father, she found that he was passed out as usual. Drunk again.

She put on her favorite sweater dress and left for her grandmother's house. Her father wouldn't wake until just before lunch anyway.

After a big hug, Francesca fried an egg for Gia. "*Sirenetta*, will you go back to school in January? I think you should be with children your age."

"No, *Nonna*. I need to help Papa in the casino. I want to learn the business. People study to learn what they want to do, and I already know."

"You do not know everything, Gia. A young woman should not be around drunks and gamblers all day."

"I have already seen worse."

Francesca hugged Gia's head to her chest, saying a silent prayer for her granddaughter to find peace. "Why not run along to Vittore's shop? I know he has a gift for you."

Gia buttoned up her coat and set off for the barbershop. The bell jingled as she pushed through the door.

"*Tesoro mio!*" Vittore cried out, racing to pick her up. "Father in the sky! Each day you become more beautiful. Sit, sit."

There were no customers in yet. He reached for his scissors and held her long hair high up off her head. "Today we cut all of this hair and maybe we give you a look like that Billie Jean movie. Very short like a boy, and then only one long, long earring!"

Gia scrunched up her face and shook her head a bunch. "Braid it!"

"Do not let my regulars see me doing this. The old men will want to grow out their hair and have me plait it up like Heidi!"

He massaged her scalp and then gave her a lovely fishtail braid. After he finished, he reached into the drawer and presented her with a white box wrapped in a pink bow. Her eyes were wide with delight and she tugged at the box and uncovered a silver barrette in the shape of a clamshell with inlaid pearls and filigree scrolls.

"So beautiful! Please, put it in." She elongated her neck, and Vittore clipped it in, above her ear. "I love it! Thank you!" Gia squeezed him so tightly he felt he might burst.

"Where is your father?" She cast her eyes to the floor. Vittore sucked his teeth and sighed. "Tonight I come to your house and cook you dinner. A big fish!" She crossed her arms and frowned at him. "Fine! Then pasta. You are exactly like your mother, *tesoro mio.*"

Kissing him on the cheek as she departed, she floated out onto the street feeling quite revived. Catching a glimpse of herself in a store window, Gia smiled at her reflection. She was so distracted that she smacked right into a boy, and they both tripped and fell.

"I am so sorry," she said, gathering herself together.

"I don't speak Italian," he replied in English. He was wearing a baseball cap with an LA logo and a red vest like Marty McFly. He looked about twenty.

"I speak English, a little."

"Cool," he said, "my name is Josh." He put out his hand for her to shake. She took it, awkwardly.

"Gia."

"Great to meet you, Gia. I'm lost. I'm trying to find San Marco. Can you tell me how to get there?"

"I will take you, if you like."

"That would be rad."

She giggled. "First, maybe we have a caffè latte?"

"Sure, okay. I'm not meeting my friends until ten-thirty."

"*Perfetto, andiamo.*" She led him through the streets and over bridges, and just before they reached San Marco, she paused at the end of a bridge in front of the Hotel Bauman. Her stomach churned sour as she thought of her mother and that monster, where they were entombed many meters below. "Today is my birthday."

"No way! Happy birthday! Coffee's on me."

"This is my favorite place," she said, pointing to the hotel. "Maybe we have the caffè latte here?"

"Cool, yeah, why not."

They ordered coffee in the lobby lounge. When the mugs were delivered, she took hers and stood up. "I will go to the patio. You come with me?"

"Okay, sure."

She steered him to the back of the hotel. The bar was closed, so they slipped onto the terrace without anyone noticing them—it was too cold for al fresco dining, so the patio was empty.

Suddenly, Gia grabbed his hand and pulled him into a secluded corner and kissed him. He kissed her back. At once, she realized that they were standing on top of the cave. Gia opened her mouth and put her tongue in Josh's. He pushed her against the wall as she let out a squeal and put her hands in his hair. Pressing his face into hers, she kissed him deeply.

He pulled away for a second and played with the zipper on his red vest. "Woah, that was unexpected," he said.

She grabbed the zipper instinctively and closed the vest all the way up to his neck. Gia kissed him again, and he closed his eyes as she kept hers open. Then, she raised her arm very slowly. Under her skin she felt the tickle of her sharp gills and reflected back to July, to the boat. Her mother had sliced diagonally.

Her skin separated, and the iridescent, white gills emerged. She thrust her tongue hard into the American's mouth, and he moaned. She could feel his erection on her leg. He'd let her do anything to him right now, and she knew that. She could feel him succumbing to her, and that felt so good. Allowing her heart to knock fifteen or so times in her chest, Gia then moved quickly and she sliced into his neck deeply, cutting him from left to right above his Adam's apple.

He opened his eyes and grabbed his neck, shock and disbelief on his face. Blood rushed out of him and onto his vest. Gia watched in awe for a few seconds as he bled out, and when a boat flew by, she hugged him to her chest. He was gargling and shaking. She felt like kissing him again, but she was worried they'd be seen. Together, they stumbled over to the railing by the water.

Gia shoved him in and then dropped into the water after him. He was still alive and made a sad effort to swim. No matter, she held onto his vest and kept him underwater. He struggled, but once her tail came in, he was no match for her.

She dragged him down beneath the rocks with ease.

He died halfway down, and a trail of blood swayed behind him. Once they were in her cave, she filled his pockets with rocks and he sank to the bottom. She would come back later with a fresh chain. Admittedly, she was feeling so much better now.

40

L *a Nonna* stacked the cash in her safe and locked it away.

"So?" Gia said, tapping her foot on the leg of the chair in her fixer's office.

"We have a slight conflict of interest."

Gia rolled her hand, indicating that the old woman should hurry it up.

"Another client contacted me. He has asked me to keep his name confidential. Apparently, they have your cousin."

Gia squeezed her eyebrows together. "Why did you tell me to come here to Rome? Can we not conduct business over the phone as usual?"

"Look." *La Nonna* opened the cover of her iPad and pressed play on a video. On the screen was Kostas, and he was looking into the camera like it was a hostage video, except he was not tied up.

A man in the background asked questions in Italian, which Kostas answered.

"Who is Gia Acquaviva?"

"My cousin," Kostas said.

"What do you want everyone to know about her?"

"She has many secrets."

"Like what?"

"The biggest one you will not believe."

"Try me."

"She has a tail."

The man behind the camera busted up laughing. "What? Like the devil? Like a rabbit?"

"Like a mermaid."

"Are you high?"

"Of course not. I've got one, too."

The man became hysterical again before the camera cut and the screen went black.

La Nonna put her hand out. "There is more," she said.

The camera came back to life, but there was some commotion. Water was running from a hose into a baby pool. Kostas came into the frame, bare-legged, and cupping his hands over his manhood. He eased down into the water. In a minute or so, below his big belly, something incredible began to appear. Legs zipped in, scales poked out, and then, there it was: His tail, brown and lackluster, flopped over the edge of the blow-up pool.

"Jesus Christ," the man behind the camera whispered. Several men wearing masks approached Kostas and touched his tail.

"I am suddenly craving sushi!" one squawked.

Then the footage stopped abruptly.

La Nonna closed the tablet and put it off to the side.

"I think you can understand why I wanted to see you in person."

Gia cocked her head to the side. "Come on. That is obviously special effects. You cannot believe that is real."

"I do actually."

"Absurd," sniffed Gia.

"Gia, how did you get all those bodies under the hotel?"

"Scuba."

La Nonna crossed her fingers and lifted her hands under her chin. "I am on your side. But hear me, I know this is not a fake thing. My client called me, and I saw it with my own eyes. Lucky for you, they are willing to make a deal."

Gia narrowed her gaze.

"A trade," *La Nonna* said, looking intently at her client. "They will dispose of this recording and your cousin, but they want partnership in your casinos."

"Drug money? Not interested," Gia replied with conviction.

"Then they will leak this recording."

"So what? It does not prove anything about me."

"Question: The American man did not return with you to Italy. Are you together?"

"No," Gia closed her eyes. "That is finished."

"Then you do not have his parents to shield you anymore."

"I am really losing patience with you." Gia leaned forward. "Why am I paying you enormous sums of money? You cannot seem to keep me out of the press or protect me."

La Nonna smacked her lips. "Have you been called by the police for questioning?"

"Obviously not."

"Am I a publicist, Gia? Did you not think that perhaps murdering a Hollywood star might kick up a bit of dust, *angioletta*?"

Gia eyed the old woman and tried to consider her next move. "Here is what I propose to your client. Five million for my cousin and the tape."

"I think this will not be enough," *La Nonna* inhaled through tight lips, "but I will present your offer. Wait outside please."

Gia excused herself and took to leaning on the wall in the dim hallway. The smell of toasted almonds and caramelized sugar snaked through the floorboards. The thought of her grandmother baking treats for the holidays passed through her mind and melancholy spread like a fog in her brain.

Tomorrow was her birthday, and she dreaded the idea of being alone. Even laughing with Vittore would not clear her sense of emptiness, loneliness. She missed Cameron more than she had expected she would.

Maybe I do love him, she thought. *Is this what heartbreak feels like?*

He'd scarcely left her mind since her jet took off from New York more than a week ago. She longed for things to be different, but maybe they were simply not meant to be together.

Especially now that she had yet another thing to concern herself with.

Sinking Kostas to the bottom of some body of water would have been much more satisfying for her and simple, but unfortunately, offing him was not an option.

What would happen to her if her Greek family turned their backs?

There was no other choice. She had to get Kostas and bring him home. Then again, her Greek family would absolutely not accept having their existence exposed, so what would happen to him for betraying his kind? Not since ancient times had Mermaid mingled openly with Man. Kostas and his idiotic choice to reveal the family secret put everyone in jeopardy.

La Nonna interrupted Gia's train of thought and signaled her back into the office, closing the door.

"*Allora*," *La Nonna* began, "you have a difficult choice in front of you. My other client wants ten million... for your cousin *or* for the tape."

"Pardon?"

"Either you get the recording and your cousin conveniently disappears... or you can have your cousin alive and unharmed, but my client keeps the recording."

Gia's mouth dropped "This will not do. You must call him back and increase the offer. Twenty million for both."

"I am so sorry, Gia. He is very adamant. If you do not want him as a partner in the casinos, then that is the only deal he is willing to make."

Gia covered her mouth and thought long and hard. This was quite a mess. There had to be some other way to get rid of the recording. If *La Nonna* couldn't help, then Gia would have to think of something on her own.

"I choose my cousin."

"I see," *La Nonna* stared off at nothing for a while, seeming truly worried. "Then I will make the arrangements. But, Gia, I do not like this agreement for you," *La Nonna* sighed. "Please consider this again. Why not just let my client take care of him for you?"

"It is not the way. I have to bring Kostas to my family."

La Nonna shook her head and began to wrap up the details. "Day after tomorrow I will deliver your cousin. Where do you want him?"

"Athens."

"Fine. And if my client releases the recording?"

"Would he do that?"

"I hope not, but I cannot be sure."

"No one in their right mind is going to see that tape and believe it. Mermaids are silly fairy tales." Her breath was shallow as she spoke, and she shuddered. Inside her arms, she could feel her sharp gills retreating below her muscles, which produced intense pain and made her grimace.

41

Gia woke up in her palazzo alone. Maybe Vittore was right when he told her that her house was an oversized marble coffin; it felt oppressive on a rainy morning. She huffed and rolled out of bed. Fifty years old today––and pregnant, wow. Her grandmother in Santorini birthed her last child at ninety. How the woman managed that, Gia had no idea.

As she undressed for a bath, Gia wondered if Harper was watching her now, surveilling her via a live feed from a non-descript, albeit sneaky, app. The kind that one might log into from a phone's calculator, like a jealous husband.

Gia bitterly reflected on the fact that Harper had definitely not dropped the beat. Every night she devoted a hefty chunk of her news hour to "Nico and Associates." However, Gia was hopeful as interest from the general public seemed to be waning. A new story about a missing Florida woman and her young daughter was the latest fascination.

Driving her boat over to Vittore's, Gia thought it more prudent to stay off the streets and keep a lower profile. In addition to the fact that she was surely being followed by Harper's PI, she was somewhat fearful of radical keyboard warriors trolling online message boards for conspiracies... the sort of people who might spend hours comparing the original security footage that showed her against the Royce-doctored version starring Jessica Joyce.

The thought of countless pairs of anonymous eyes ogling her made her feel uneasy and detached from herself. She had the bizarre sensation of being an outside observer, as if her body wasn't hers at all. In this disturbing mental state, she felt like a drone, like the "real" Gia was somewhere else, somewhere very far away, manipulating her. Gia had found herself moving in an odd, robotic manner and absent-mindedly smiling at inappropriate moments. Without much interaction with people in the last few weeks, she had forgotten what a normal person was like. How did a normal person smile? Cry? Show just the right amount of empathy? Most importantly, how would a normal person act if they were perfectly innocent?

She passed under a bridge as a couple kissed inside a gondola. Remembering her gondola ride with Cameron, the corners of her mouth sagged.

The unwelcome picture of him riding the elevator in his building down to Zeus and picking up some other woman flooded her mind. She imagined him doing to someone new all the things he'd done to her. Sour acid swished in her stomach, and she cupped what she imagined was the baby.

Cameron had not texted, not called, not even attempted to communicate since she left his parents' home on Thanksgiving.

Why?

She blew every molecule of air out of her lungs and resolved to stop thinking of him for the rest of the day. She would especially not think about the sex.

Good god, the sex.

Inside Vittore's tiny apartment, she lifted a table leg and wedged some paper to stop the table from wobbling. He patted her on the back and handed her a bowl of mushroom risotto. She winced before telling him what she needed to say.

"*Methusalamme*," she swizzled her spoon in the bowl like a kid. He always made the dish extra creamy for her. "I want to tell you something, but I need you to promise me that you will not be angry with me."

"*Tesoro mio!* This is a devil bargain. I do not make devil bargains."

She glanced down at her tummy and raised her shirt to show the tiniest little bump. "I am pregnant, Vittore." The old man fell into his chair and began to pray.

"Gia, wonderful! Wonderful, fantastic! You make me so happy, like today is my birthday and not your birthday. Let me get some wine. No! No, you cannot have wine! A baby! Ah! Father in the sky! What a blessing! Maybe I will go out to buy a few sweets to celebrate this beautiful occasion."

Gia exhaled and laid down her spoon. "I am not sure I will keep it."

"Pardon?" Color drained from the old man's face.

"A baby is a lot to take on by myself."

"You have me!"

"I love you so much, but you are very old already, *amore*."

"No! You have money! You can have an army of nannies for the baby if you like. You cannot kill this child."

"Vittore!"

"What!? That is what they do, is it not? The doctor removes the baby and in doing so, kills it."

"I did not take you for an old-fashioned anti-abortionist!"

"Of course I am not, Gia, but please! Your circumstances are very different. You are not some young girl. No! You are a grown woman, and you can take care of this child, but you simply do not wish to compromise your lifestyle, and I think this is wrong. I am sorry to say, but yes, I feel this is wrong."

"Unbelievable. This is my right, you know. This is my body, and I can choose what I do with it."

Vittore stared down at his bowl, holding back tears.

"Ha!" Gia yelled, pushing back from the table. "Happy birthday to me! What a way to celebrate!" She held her eyes on Vittore, but he didn't look up at her. "I think I will leave now."

The old man nibbled without much interest and muttered, "This is your body... you take it wherever you like."

His words irritated Gia very much. She made a lot of noise walking away, hoping he would call out for her, but he did not—not even when she slammed the door behind her.

Once she was in the street, she felt overcome with a tingling sensation that began in her arms and spread like a thousand painful stings through her body, resting finally in her chest. She was so heavy on top that she felt she might tip over. Taking steps felt like pulling her feet through mud, and with every second that passed, the pressure in her chest ached more deeply.

She couldn't catch her breath. She opened her mouth to let in more air, but instead, out came a wail. It sounded like the violent ripping of a metal sheet. She had that strange dissociative feeling again, and the real Gia floated off to the side, while her robot body broke down.

Gia braced herself against a wall and out rushed a flood of tears. She tried holding her breath to stop the flow, but it did nothing. She gagged from the loss of air before she collapsed into the street and sobbed uncontrollably.

Her mind raced and raced. What was happening? Why cry now, after so long? Were these pregnancy hormones? She hadn't shed a single tear since her mother died all those years ago.

Gia barely noticed when someone crouched over her. She was far, far away by then, simultaneously lost in her panic and completely divorced from it.

"Come," said the voice. A hand wrapped around hers. It was a warm and bony hand, with papery thin skin: Vittore's hand.

Gia managed somehow to pull herself off the ground and lumber back to the old man's place. He sat her down on the bed and stroked her hair while she cried. Inside her mind, she found herself tumbling backward, down, down, down, like Alice in the rabbit hole. Thoughts flew past her at an incredible speed. Flashes. It was as though she were passing miniature movie theaters playing highlights from the worst moments of her life.

Her mother's bleeding head. Her father's bloated and broken body after his deadly boat crash. Her mother decomposing into bones in her underwater grave. The eyes of the man who killed her mother being eaten by a fish. The moment her grandmother's ashes were flung into the lagoon. The look of devastation on Cameron's face as she left him—

And then, just like that, at the sight of Cameron's face, Gia's floating body came to a rest inside the cavern of her mind. It was suspended, as if held up by the softest cloud. Everywhere around her, she saw Cameron's face, smiling and laughing. Kissing her, making love to her. And she felt safe.

The crying stopped, and Gia became aware of her head laying on Vittore's rounded shoulder. She stayed there a moment more, although his shirt was very wet and sticky.

Finally, Gia took a deep breath and focused on Vittore as she asked him with a weak and quivering voice, "Will you come to London with me?"

* * *

GIA TRIED to drink a bourbon on the jet for strength, but Vittore put a stop to it. She chattered her teeth and cracked her knuckles, and when none of that calmed her down, she began pacing up and down the aisle.

"*Tesoro mio!* Please, you will give me an anxiety attack if you do not sit and relax yourself. Come, tell me, what will you say to him?"

Gia smooshed her face into a rodent-like grimace and shook her head.

The truth was she had no idea what to say to Cameron.

She didn't even know if he was in London. It was entirely possible that this trip was carelessly tossing jet fuel into the English Channel.

And if he were home, would he want to see her? Should she call him when they landed? Text him? What if he had another woman at his place?

Maybe this was a foolish and ill-conceived plan. But she could not help herself. Gia had never wanted anything more than she had wanted to see Cameron in that moment. She wished she could snap her fingers and have him appear. Why had she left him alone in New York? How stupid!

After the agonizing flight, Vittore encouraged Gia to call Cameron, so she did.

It went to voicemail.

Fuck! Maybe this was all for nothing!

She asked the driver to speed up. Finally, they arrived at his building. There was a long line in front of Zeus, which made her happy and distracted her for a split-second. They entered the lobby that led to the residences, and she walked up to the bespeckled doorman and cleared her throat.

"We are here to see Cameron Langley," she said.

"Is he expecting you?"

"No."

He lifted a telephone and rang Cam's apartment. "Sir, you have two guests." The doorman peered over the thin rim of his glasses and said, "Your names, please?"

"Tell him that Miss Acquaviva and Mr. Cantalupi wish very much to speak with him."

He dutifully repeated what she had iterated, and then to Cameron he said, "Very good, sir." He hung up the phone. Gia thought she might pass out. Were they cleared to enter or not?

"Ahem," Gia reminded the doorman of her presence.

"Mr. Langley will be down in a moment. Please have a seat."

Vittore folded himself into a low, velvet chair, but Gia stayed standing. After ten or so minutes and several false starts with someone else exiting the elevator, Cameron finally emerged.

Gia licked her lips and held her breath. Cameron raised his head and locked eyes with her.

His expression was completely neutral.

He walked over to Vittore and shook his hand first. "Good to see you," he said.

In response, Vittore jerked Cameron's hand into him, and

Cameron came tumbling into the seat. The old man threw his arms around the younger man and let out a small whimper.

Cameron backed up awkwardly. He looked at Gia—just looked, not smiled, not glowered. He simply observed her standing there and didn't say a word.

"Ahh..." Gia began unsteadily. "Today is my birthday."

"I'm aware," Cameron replied.

"Might we come upstairs and speak with you?" she asked him.

Cameron held his breath before speaking. "I'm not sure that's a good idea. I—"

"She is keeping the baby!" Vittore blurted out, before covering his mouth with his hand.

Cameron's eyes went wide. "Let's have this conversation in private."

As they rode up to the penthouse, Vittore held Gia's hand the whole time as she closed her eyes and inhaled Cameron's cologne. She was sure he could hear her heart beating. All she wanted to do was kiss him and not stop for days.

Cameron led them into the kitchen and took out a bottle of sparkling water from the fridge. Gia smiled to herself.

Maybe Europe was finally reforming his tap-water ways?

They took their places around his kitchen table. Cameron sat in silence until Gia spoke. "I am very sorry, Cameron..." Gia forgot what she wanted to say. She had no concrete plan, after all, only the idea to see him and talk, but where could she even begin?

"About which part?"

She swallowed a sip of water. "I should not have left you at your parents' house. I realize that now."

"Okay." His tone sounded dismissive, blasé even. Gia felt as if she had been stabbed in the gut.

"I suppose..." Gia was losing her train of thought again. This was not going well at all. "Perhaps I should not have left at all. I—"

"Correct," Cameron interrupted. "You should not have left. Do you know what it took for me to ask my parents for help? I've never, never done that. Never! I have tried for my whole life to be independent and not rely on them for anything. Because there are always strings attached to their help. But I pushed past what was good for me, and I went to them for you and our baby. I showed you, really showed you, that I was there for you... and you left me!"

"I am so sorry."

"You ripped my goddamn heart out of my chest, you know that right?"

Gia bit her lip.

"Please," Vittore interjected, "if I may share with you some wisdom from a very old man?" Cameron angled his head toward Vittore and nodded. "My Gia is special. She is not like other women."

"Vittore," Gia said, "it is all right. I can speak for myself."

"I know, *tesoro mio*, but I believe there are many things you may find too difficult to say." He took Cameron's hand in his and looked into his soul. "Gia has pain inside that you cannot imagine, young man. I have known her since before she was born, when she was a little fish swimming in her mamma's belly. I held her in my arms when she was born, and I have loved her like my own beautiful daughter ever since. She was a sweet young thing. But something broke inside her, Cameron, when her mamma died. She was only fifteen years old then. And then her papa, my Luca, he died this very night, on Gia's birthday, thirty-four years ago."

"Thirty-four years ago?" Cameron searched the old man's eyes for answers. "But—"

"I love you, Cameron," Gia whispered, "and it is time for me to be honest with you."

Cameron frowned, and deep lines in his forehead settled in like sleeping dogs.

"Like you, Cameron, I have tried to be independent, but it was out of necessity. Because I was forced to be an adult after my mother was murdered. My father drank himself nearly to death, and when that did not do the trick, he rowed his gondola into a *vaporetto*. It was my sixteenth birthday. So, that makes me fifty years old today."

"That's not possible..."

"But it is, you see. There are many things about me that you do not know. Things you must know if you are to be the father of our child."

"Maybe I don't want that."

"*Amore*," Gia scooted closer to him. "I know you do. I could hear it in your voice when you talked about sending the baby to school, and I could see it in your eyes when you kissed me. We love each other, and we deserve a chance to make this work."

"But you keep *lying* to me, Gia."

"Sì, sì," Vittore agreed. "You are not wrong. Gia has lied many times to you and many times to many other people. But there is a reason. A good reason. Tell him, Gia, tell him why."

"I have never told anyone this, so, I... I am not sure how to say it."

"Tell me now, Gia," Cameron said, reaching out for her hand. "Tell me before I change my mind."

"My mother is from Greece."

"Yes, I know. You mentioned that."

"But what I did not tell you is that she is actually from the sea."

"What? Is that some kind of Italian expression? I think there's something being lost in translation."

"No, Cameron, my mother was born *in the sea* off the coast of Santorini. She was born in the colony," Gia swallowed hard, steeling herself for what was to come next, "in the mermaid colony."

Her words hung in the air, and for a moment, silence enveloped the room.

"Ahahahaha!" Cameron broke the tense air with his thick laughter. "You really shouldn't pull my leg like this. Come on. Don't make jokes, Gia."

Vittore creaked forward. "She means what she says."

"Enough, enough. I know you guys like to kid around. This is serious. I wanna know the reason why you lied to me."

"This is the reason, Cameron," Gia said, narrowing her eyes.

"That your mother's a mermaid," he retorted.

"Yes. And I am also a mermaid."

"Like in 'Splash'," he continued, rolling his eyes this time.

"Yes."

"Cameron," Vittore said, "this is absolutely true. I have kept the secret since her father and I pulled her mother from the sea. Believe me, I thought mermaids were the subject of silly children's stories. But they are real. Gia is my *sirenetta*."

"Hold on, hold on." Cameron waved his hands across the table. "Time out. Are you serious right now?"

"For the love of God, Cameron. My mother was a mermaid. I am a mermaid, and this baby inside me is a mermaid. Yes."

"The... baby..."

"Yes, the baby is a mermaid, that is how this works."

Cameron sat in his chair, looking like tiny stars were circling his head, as if someone had hit him upside the head with a cast-iron pan.

"Come with me."

Cameron watched Gia glide across his apartment to his bathroom. She filled the tub with water, and removed her clothes, sitting on the edge of the tub, dipping her feet in.

Cameron wandered toward her, in a sort of dazed state. When he reached her, he saw her feet morph into what looked like feathers, pearly white and translucent. The scales along where her ankles and calves would have been shimmered and shone like opals in bright sunshine. He reached down and touched her tail. It was slippery, but not unpleasant. It felt like the wet skin of a boa constrictor, lightly ridged and elegant.

He ran his hand along the edge of her tail, and she tickled him and splashed water on his face, earning her the beginning of a smile.

"I'm gonna need a minute to process all of this," he said, still fixated on the miracle in front of his eyes.

42

DECEMBER 8TH

Inside Gia's bathroom Cameron pointed at various items, singing the iconic lyrics from *The Little Mermaid* that Ariel belts out in her cave full of human knick-knacks.

Gia snuck up on him from behind and took his razor out of his hand, arching his head back toward her. She began to shave him, gold blades cutting neat lines in the shaving cream like a snowplow.

"You may find this shocking," Gia said, as she scraped his neck, "but I have missed your performances."

"How could you not? I'm *this close* to going pro. Just waiting for my big break."

Gia laid her head on his bare chest and breathed him in: Byredo fragrance, steam from the shower, and the smell that was uniquely his—something like fresh-baked bread and a buttery leather sofa.

Uncharted territory she was sailing in now.

Never had she opened herself up to a man in this way—she had never felt the need and never wanted to. But resting against his strong body, she felt satisfied in a new way. Indeed, it was a sort of elation. Maybe this is what regular people experienced when they felt connected to someone else.

Surely this was love?

The *"I can't live without you"* feelings had smacked her down rather fiercely just the day before. But what now? Would they go to birthing classes and buy a bassinet and take Christmas card photos together for the next eighteen or twenty years?

"What do you want to do today?" Cam asked her, dissipating her deep thoughts.

"Are you not going into the office?"

"Gia, remember my mother threatening to call the owner of the bank to ask for time off? She did it. I'm on paid leave until after New Year's Day. I attempted to go back in last week, and my boss called his boss's boss, and the three of them took me for a steak lunch, got me drunk, and sent me home with a friendly warning not to return until after the holidays. I'm bored to death. Should we pick up Vittore from my apartment and take him to the National Portrait Gallery or maybe to the movies?"

Gia winced. "I have to go, actually."

"Go where?"

"Ah..." She wasn't sure where this new truth-telling deal between them began and ended. Was she really supposed to tell him everything? All the time? "Do you remember my cousin Kostas?"

"The one from the club?"

"I am having a rather serious problem with him."

"Okay..."

"I have to take him home today."

"To Venice?"

She inhaled through her teeth, "To Greece."

"Greece!"

"Mmhmm."

"Wait... wait..." Cameron ran a washcloth under hot water and cleansed his face. "Not... to Santorini?"

Gia nodded, face plastered with a strange smile-frown.

"So, there are guy mermaids?"

"Of course!"

"Oh my God! Okay? Well... uh... I guess I just never thought about that as being a possibility. Not that..." he scrunched up his mouth and mumbled the next bit, "not that I considered mermaids in general as, you know, a real thing." He started packing his toiletries into his Dopp kit. "So, what's going on with Kostas the merman exactly?"

"Mmmm," Gia's voice was sing-song and unsure, "I guess you could call it... blackmail?"

"What?!"

"*Amore*, please do not ask me all the details. I am enjoying this time with you, and we just came together, and I truly do not want to upset you."

"Woah, woah, woah. Now you *have* to tell me what's going on."

Gia pressed her fingers hard into her temples and stared at the countertop. Cameron craned his head under hers and dragged her eyes up to his.

"So?" he said. "Spill it. What?"

"Fine. He has been coordinating with a Sicilian crime family to steal money from me and is now threatening to tell the media the existence of mermaids—he made a tape, showing his tail. But I have it under control. I am picking him up tonight in Athens."

"A crime family? So, you're saying you have to pick up your merman cousin from the mafia?"

"Not from the mafia directly. I have an intermediary."

"Which is who exactly?"

"Cameron, stop."

"Oh no! I don't think so. No, no, nope. I'm not letting a pregnant woman walk into a dangerous situation like that. No way. We're calling the police."

"The police?" she scoffed. "Think about this for a second. *Amore*, no one calls the police on the mafia. That is not the way to handle this sort of thing. And, if I try to do anything strange, they will release the tape to the press. I cannot let that happen. I have to protect myself, protect our baby."

"You sound like my mother."

Gia shrugged. Cameron cursed silently to himself.

"I'm going with you then! Not taking no for an answer."

"I will be perfectly safe. I have everything sorted," Gia insisted.

"Forget it. From now on, if you get on that jet, I'm coming with you."

43

What a different plane ride it was when compared to the day before; Cameron held Gia's hand and she rested her head on his shoulder. Vittore sat opposite of them feeling quite satisfied with himself for having done his part to bring them together and secure a happier future for his beloved Gia. As the landing gear dropped, Gia felt the muscles in Cameron's neck constrict. When they hit the tarmac, his hand was sweating.

"*Amore*," she whispered in his ear, "everything will be just fine."

Her jet angled into a large airplane hangar where another, smaller jet was parked. The other plane, matte black in color, featured a sleek design with a vintage feel, sort of like a fighter jet. Gia had never seen one like it.

Sauntering down the jet's steps was *La Nonna*. Gustav, Gia's flight attendant, opened the hatch and stepped outside to give Gia privacy. *La Nonna* passed him on her way in. When the old woman saw that Gia had brought two guests she flinched and flashed Gia a stern look. Onlookers weren't part of the bargain.

"Where is Kostas?" Gia demanded.

"Who are your friends?" *La Nonna* deflected.

Vittore stood and tipped his head to her. "Vittore Cantalupi. I knew your father. We met on many occasions in the past. He helped me with legal matters several times."

She tilted her head to the side to acknowledge that nothing more needed to be said before she turned her attention to Cameron. "And you, Casanova?"

"I'm with Gia."

"Tell me something I cannot see with my own two, aging eyes," she chortled.

"This is Cameron," Gia said, stroking his stiff arm.

"Ah, how nice. The lovers have reunited! If only we had time for a celebration drink. *Bene, allora...* shall we begin with business?"

"We are not here to have a party," Gia said, voice becoming shrill. "So yes. Bring Kostas to me."

"He is next door."

"On the other plane?" Gia asked.

La Nonna edged in toward Gia and lowered her voice, "My client would like to speak with you."

Gia bristled, "This was not what was agreed."

"Unfortunately," *La Nonna* replied, "this is a new and non-negotiable term. Shall we?"

Cameron put his arm out across Gia's belly to prevent her from moving. "I'll go," he said.

La Nonna popped her eyes out and cackled. "Hilarious!"

Cameron rose, and she stopped laughing.

Staring at Gia, she became serious. "This will not be allowed. Now, come *piccolina*, before my client loses his patience. He becomes rather unfriendly when he is kept waiting."

Cam's jaw tensed as he watched Gia stand. He spoke in a low tone to her through gritted teeth. "What the fuck, Gia? This is not safe."

She leaned in and kissed him under his ear and whispered, "I will be back in three little snaps of a lobster claw."

"If you're not on the jet steps in five minutes, I'm getting the pilot and coming over there for you."

"That will not be necessary." She ran her fingers through his hair, kissed him quickly, and was out the door.

The two women climbed the extended stairs and entered the black jet. Inside were four men: Kostas, who was wedged between the two beefy men she'd seen in her London club, and in the back of the plane, behind a glossy black table was an extremely tanned silver fox who looked like Cary Grant.

"*Chaíromai pou se vlépo*, Kosta," Gia said, telling her cousin it was nice to see him while her words dripped with rage. He turned his head to look out the window at nothing.

"*Signorina* Acquaviva," the mob boss crooned, "please join me." She slank into a black suede chair across from him. "Tell me, *bella sirenetta*, is your fishtail more elegant than that lazy motherfucker's? It must be. Maybe you can show me later, ah?"

"Do you mind getting to the point of this little meeting? I have plans this evening," Gia said, poised at the edge of her seat.

Although Gia could not see *La Nonna*, she could feel the old woman shifting nervously behind her.

"Why not cancel your plans and fly to Sicily with me?" The silver fox said, turning up the corner of his mouth.

"You have your funds, do you not?" she replied to him.

"I do."

"Then I believe our business is concluded."

"*Wooooo woot*," he whistled. "The lady is in such a rush." He leaned forward and put his elbows on the table. "I would like a little dessert, you see. Something to sweeten the meal. I am not finding enough satisfaction in our deal." Gia scowled at him, but he continued, undeterred. "Your club in Amalfi has always been a favorite of mine. It would be the perfect accompaniment to my other holdings."

Gia pinched her lips, "I was very clear with our lawyer *Signora* Sapienti that I have no interest in taking on partners. I must very kindly reject your offer."

"Mmm. That is a shame. I had hoped we could come to a suitable arrangement." He sighed and shrugged, "A man has to try, does he not?" He winked at her then. "Off you go, little fish. Do let Donatella know if the waters become too hot for you to swim in all alone." He signaled for *La Nonna*. "Donatella darling, please escort *Signorina* Acquaviva to her plane, along with *Signor* Jumbo Shrimp."

"As you wish." With that, *La Nonna* called Kostas over and took Gia by the arm, ushering both he and Gia out the door.

44

DECEMBER 8TH

To the west of Santorini, a short boat ride away is *Nisí Margaritarión*, Pearl Island. Its tall, white ridges look like the back of a polar bear bent into the Aegean Sea, swatting at fish. The surface is largely uninhabited, save for a skinny, white lighthouse and a small patch of Cypress forest around it. The cliffs on the south side of the island conceal a half-moon cove and deep blue waters, which lead to a network of underwater caves.

Gia splashed a small motorboat through the waves, trying as best she could to keep the ride smooth for Vittore. The old man was shining ear to ear; it was always his dream to return to Greece and see the splendid mermaids again. The waxing moon offered only a little light, and the human men were freezing as they were lashed by the December winds.

Vittore and Cameron wore wetsuits and covered themselves with blankets. Getting the scuba suit over Vittore's crooked body had been a real feat, and Gia wasn't entirely sure if her sweet old friend was up for the dive. Kostas, on the other hand, sulked and wrapped himself into a ball.

Once they reached the cove, Gia spotted her grandparents waiting on the beach, holding a lantern. Below them, the sand reflected light

like the inside of a shell. The name of the island came from the frag-
ments of pearl that created its unique, glimmering beach. Triton and
Xania were a sight, like a pair of attractive sea ghosts. They both had
long, flowing hair like Gia, but theirs had turned grey many moons
ago. Xania's still showed a whimper of the roaring red that it once had
been, while Triton's dark grey mane looked almost blue. The couple
was tall and both a bit gaunt, in the way that aging athletes sometimes are. They wore mesh caftans, as most of the colony's mermaids
did.

Gia tied the boat up inside a small cave and helped Vittore and
Cameron off onto the beach. Vittore grabbed Cameron's hand and
recited a poem he remembered, "Into the great unknown we go, to
swim, to know, to see how the tiny fish grow!"

Cameron shivered and pulled his blanket tighter around him,
trying to cover his ears, which he felt were due to fall off any second
now. Gia hugged him and rubbed her hands over his ears without
him asking, which felt really soothing and nice.

"Do not worry, *amore*," she said quietly, "below the island are
many hot springs. Soon you will be very warm."

"Thank Christ," Cameron replied. "I don't think I've ever been
this cold."

Gia kissed her grandparents and embraced them. They
exchanged loving words in an archaic tongue, a mix of Greek and
ocean songs, and mystic whispers. Then they welcomed Kostas home
—but in a much less affectionate manner. Gia made Kostas retrieve
the scuba gear from the boat and help the humans strap in. The
group then slid into the dark water and dove below the waves.

Gia held onto Cameron and Vittore, leading the way. The glowing
light of the four mermaids' eyes illuminated the caves and the men
took in the incredible scenery around them. Pink, blue, and green
rock formations dripped from the ceiling above their heads into the
water like melting candles. Cameron felt as though he'd been
kidnapped by extraterrestrials and was now wandering a foreign
planet. He watched Gia's white tail swish in the water, propelling
them forward at a good speed. Kostas was behind them, brown tail

flicking lazily. Rounding up the back were his grandparents. Triton's tail was white and shiny like Gia's, but Xania's was emerald green.

And Gia had been right. The water was perfect, not boiling; it was the temperature of a hot bath after having settled. Vittore's body liked being underwater. His back seemed to unkink itself a bit, and he felt no pain. In fact, he felt rather young again. Maybe there was magic in the water.

After some minutes, they were not sure how many, they arrived at a startling location: the carved entrance to a small, subaquatic village. A pathway curved out of the water and up onto dry rock to become the town's main street. Mermaids walked on two legs in this strange and elaborate collection of caves. The main avenue was lit with thousands of candelabras hanging from the ceiling and lining the path were alien-looking crystals the size of pumpkins. They glowed in pastel tones. The white walls of the caves were ornately chiseled into some form of hieroglyphics, which had been decorated with what looked like watercolors.

Cameron marveled at the beauty around him. The cavern had the look of a very holy place, a temple, but the vibe was more sensual and distinctly alive. There were several shops and a few restaurants. Voices echoed over one another, becoming a harmonic hum, and the sound made Cameron feel sleepy. He was anxious to get out of his scuba suit and settle in somewhere to let this new world wash over him.

45

Cameron glanced out the leaded glass windows in Xania's underwater mansion. There were scallop shapes in some of the panels. The room jutted out from the rest of the house and rather than any kind of art, the ceiling and the walls were fitted with varied windows—some round, some geometric, some stained glass, some simply transparent. Outside, in the water, floated odd-looking fish, bright eels, and glowing phytoplankton.

Cameron felt as though he were standing inside a Moroccan lantern that had fallen from a pirate ship and landed at the bottom of the ocean. This part of the sea was below a crevice, and it was too deep for humans to reach unassisted, and yet, here he was. The air was just as fresh as it was up on land, and he had no idea how that was possible.

The truth? Mermaid engineering: thousands of years of science and a little bit of magic.

Gia eased in behind Cameron and threaded her arms around his waist.

"*Amore*, my grandmother has arranged for us to see the doctor and check on the baby."

"Doctor? There are doctors down here?" Cameron inquired, perplexed yet amazed.

Gia giggled, "Does this look like some kind of uncivilized place to you? Certainly, we have doctors. There is a small hospital, in fact."

"Weird."

"Ah! And unlike your United States, our medical care is free!"

Cameron shook his head comically. He wasn't sure what he found more strange—the fact that mermaids existed or the fact that they'd created their own fully functioning society, more than two-thousand fathoms into the deep sea.

They ate breakfast alone in the dining room, feasting on seaweed salad, bread and nut cheese, and watermelon, all produced at the local hydroponic farm.

"This food is incredible," Cameron said, chomping away. "You've got to take me to see this farm. I don't know how you guys do all this."

"I cannot imagine anything duller than a visit to the Hanging Gardens, but I will take you, if you like," Gia relented.

"Hanging Gardens, hell yes!"

After the meal, they strolled through the house, and Gia showed Cameron around while she offered up more information about her family.

"Interestingly, Cameron, my grandparents are also in the banking business."

"What?"

"Yes, they own the colony's only bank."

"What do they trade in? Seashells?"

"Very funny. No, we actually have a fiat currency, and we use coins to buy goods. My mother invested heavily in the colony, and it has always paid hefty returns."

Cameron couldn't help but laugh, boggled by the entire situation. "I stand corrected!"

The main avenue was busy that day with trading. Shops sold clothing, food, homewares. And there were other homes carved into the rocks. The normalcy of it was shocking.

When they reached the clinic, Cameron was surprised to learn that the female doctor spoke English. "I studied gynecology at NYU," she explained.

"How?" Cameron asked, dumbfounded.

"What is it they say in New York?" the doctor answered. "How do you get to Carnegie Hall? Practice! Practice! Practice!"

"Unreal."

There was medical equipment organized around them, most of it made of brass. Modern items, but they looked like something you'd pick up at an antique shop because nothing was plastic. Mermaids had banned plastic long ago as they hated how it was polluting the ocean, making life more difficult. After all, oceans made up seventy percent of the planet. How was it fair for Man to be screwing it all up when they lived on just ten percent of occupied landmass? Humans were the worst kind of pest.

Unlike most places in the colony, the hospital had hydro-powered electricity, which was used mainly to run the medical equipment. The room was lit from those same large, glowing crystals that were on the main road, except the ones in the clinic were wall-sized panels. The doctor powered up the sonogram and felt around Gia's belly.

"She is roughly the size of a lime," the doctor said.

"It's a girl?" Cameron said, voice halting. "How can you tell?"

"See the tail pattern here? That indicates a female."

"Oh my God." His face drained of blood as he considered this new information. "Will she stay like that?" he questioned.

"Like what?" Gia asked.

"In that... form... um... so she's definitely not human?"

The doctor raised an eyebrow at him, "That is a very good thing, sir. Mermaids live at least double the lifespan of a human, sometimes more. This little mermaid looks perfectly healthy. Congratulations."

He tumbled backward onto a stool and sat, speechless.

"First baby?" The doctor asked, turning to Gia.

"Yes," she replied.

"You will need to take some supplements and special hormones since she's an inter-species child. I'll send you home with a prescription."

Cameron chewed the cuticle of his thumb and remained quiet.

How was he going to tell his parents that their first grandchild was some kind of terribly adorable sea monster?

46

Nestled next to Gia's phone inside her purse, which was stowed away in an overhead bin on the plane, Cameron's phone was glowing with an incoming call, another one, and it went to voicemail—again. Harper had been trying him for days now and getting nothing. Finally, she rang his building.

"Sky Residences," the doorman answered. "How may I assist you?"

"Hello, this is Harper Langley. I've been trying to reach my brother, Cameron Langley, for days, but he's not answering the phone. Could you check on him please?"

"Ma'am, we are not allowed to enter the residences without permission of the owner."

"What if he's missing? When did you see him last?"

"Sorry, I am not allowed to give out information on the residents."

"But I'm his sister."

"Very sorry, ma'am."

"Thanks anyway." Frustrated, Harper hung up in a huff.

For weeks, Harper's eyes had been trailing Gia but had lost sight of her on December 7th. Feeling concerned and suspicious, Harper had asked her contacts to put their ears to the ground for any whispers about Gia, and what came back was a shout.

It was imperative that she get through to Cameron ASAP as her Italian contacts had turned up a very disturbing video featuring a man who was claiming to know secrets about Gia.

As much as she despised Gia and didn't trust her, Harper was loyal to Cameron and knew she needed at least to inform him of the clip before going to Royce and Bronwyn. Harper's source had told her that the tape was absolutely shocking—guaranteed to break both cable TV and the Internet—and the seller wanted several million dollars for the full recording. The source also said there were already three interested buyers, and they all had six hours to submit a closed bid, or the tape was going to be auctioned on the Dark Web.

There wasn't enough time to fly to London to look for Cameron in the flesh, and she figured he probably wasn't there anyway.

But where the hell was he?

Part of her began to worry that he was lying somewhere with his throat cut or with a bullet in his head.

She shook off the thought, primarily because her instincts were good, and they told her that Cameron was alive somewhere and that he was most likely with Gia. Harper checked her phone and took a peek at footage from the security cameras in Gia's Venice house again. Nothing, the house was empty.

She dialed her main guy.

"It's me," she said. "I want you to put a call out to the wider team to see if they spot Gia or my brother at any of her clubs or casinos, okay? I need to hear back within the hour."

The person at the end of the line assured her he would do his best.

When they finished speaking, Harper put the phone down and leaned back in her office chair, covering her eyes with her hands.

"Where the fuck are you, Cam-Cam?"

47

"A full-on peach tree!" Cameron said, reaching for a piece of ripe fruit. "Holy shit!"

He and Gia were touring the orchard section of the Hanging Gardens. They were called that because there were seven round pods, each housing a different farming climate, hanging from a central structure, which resembled a coat hanger.

Inside the tall middle tower was a spiral staircase, leading to glass hallways, and at the edge of the hallways hung these pods, which swayed lazily in time with the ocean's movement. It was a bit dizzying.

At that moment, colony citizens were busy at work, tending to the garden. Butterflies did their jobs, too, floating in the air and pollinating the trees. The trees, and the rest of the crops, provided a good bit of oxygen to the colony. The rest was supplied via electrolysis, which split the seawater into salt for seasoning, oxygen gas for breathing, and hydrogen for sugar.

Cameron bit into the peach and juice leaked down his chin. Gia leaned in toward his face, licking it up and kissing him.

"How much longer do you want to stay?" Gia asked him.

"How about forever?"

There was still so much for him to see and learn. The dry crust of the Earth was a mere two-point-two miles north, but it may as well have been a world away.

"Can we apply for citizenship?" he laughed, only half-joking.

Gia smiled kindly. "I know it is very impressive at first, *amore*, but life down here gets very repetitive, and humans need sunshine. I cannot keep you locked at the bottom of the sea for too long."

He put the peach in her mouth and she took a bite. It was soft and ripe and its flesh rolled down her throat like wet honey.

"Let's go home and make love before we meet Vittore out for dinner," she suggested, throwing her arms around him.

Cameron made no objections.

48

DECEMBER 12TH

It was just after one o'clock in the morning when Harper parked in front of her parents' house, and she noticed that the lights were on in Bronwyn's office. She crawled out of the car and dragged her feet, one after the other.

"Good God, Harper," her father said, as she crossed the threshold of the cottage, "you look terrible."

"We lost the bid," Harper groaned, the words seemed to get caught in the back of her throat.

"Darling, we know that," Bronwyn said, sipping from a mug of hot coffee.

"Oh," Harper replied, flinging her tired body into an armchair. "Five million. Who outbids five million on a random tape that might be the equivalent of Al Capone's Vault?"

"I'll be forever grateful to your mother for not hiring Geraldo Rivera."

"Let's focus, you two," Bronwyn directed, setting her coffee onto a coaster. "Hand me the phone, dear," she said to Royce. "I'm going to call Goldie."

"Goldie Stern?" Harper asked, blinking her eyes.

"Our man says he was the winning bidder." Bronwyn scrolled

through her contacts and rang through to one of Goldie's three cell phones. It took a while, but he finally answered.

"Is that my Brownie girl?" he asked, Australian accent booming through the cell towers from Los Angeles to New York state.

"Stop it, you old flirt!" Bronwyn teased. "You may know why I'm calling... Royce and I were made aware that you purchased something this evening that is of interest to us. We were wondering if we might take it off your hands. So... what do you need from me? Are you thinking a single brownie or a whole pan?"

"Brownie, baby doll, keep your dough. This tape is too good to pass along. It's gonna make me rich."

"Goldie! You're already a billionaire, dear! Now, tell your old friend what's on the tape that's got you so interested?"

He hacked through the phone, his throat emitting gurgly sounds from a lifetime of chain-smoking. Once he cleared his throat, he rattled out a laugh. "Let's put it like this, gorgeous, every housewife in America will be glued to their TVs. This recording's up there with UFOs and unicorns. It's gonna change the world as we know it. Once we air tomorrow, I'm happy to give you the 'old friend' discount to license it for OTN. I gotta run Brownie. We're packaging a whole thing for prime time. All will be revealed in eighteen hours. I feel like the Wizard of Oz!" He coughed some more while laughing and hung up.

Bronwyn lowered the phone and with a dazed look said, "I have no idea what is on the tape, but Goldie has been bedridden in the cancer wing at Cedars-Sinai for weeks, and now he's back in the office, sounding like he just uncovered Atlantis. Whatever's on that recording has to be shocking. I don't even understand what this means for Gia and Cameron. Harper, get your friends at his network on the line. We need to know exactly what's on this tape."

49

DECEMBER 14TH

Triton set the long table for Xania. The floor beneath the living room was comprised of illuminated glass blocks, making it possible to see the aquatic life below. Around the table, there were eight cousins and several aunts and uncles, plus Gia, Vittore, and Cameron, and of course, both of Gia's grandparents. Noticeably absent: Kostas.

The last person to arrive at the big lunch was someone Vittore never expected to see, as he was sure the man had perished more than fifty years ago in Cold Currents. But no, there was Marina's Uncle Stavros, alive and well, and while he looked a bit older, he still very much resembled his 1969 self. Vittore tipped himself over and rolled uncomfortably out of the chair to greet Stavros.

"*Signor,*" Vittore said excitedly in Italian, remembering that Stavros spoke the language, "my old eyes can hardly believe what I am seeing! Father in the sky! It is you, Marina's uncle. I am Vittore, the friend of Luca. I was there all those many years ago when we found the treasure. Marina never told me that you survived!"

"Ah, that is a story for the ages. Let me tell you while we eat. Make space for me beside you." They bumped the row of cousins down, and Vittore slapped Stavros's arm with joy.

Cameron and Gia sat at the far end of the table, near her grandparents. He liked them, as far as he could tell. It was difficult to get to know them with Gia translating. Triton and Xania only spoke Greek and Atargatis, the mystical language of the sea.

Cameron munched on fruit while Gia spoke with Xania.

"He is very upset with you," Xania looked deeply into Gia's eyes, as though she was trying to extract Gia's soul. "Kostas says you are behaving in ways that are harmful to him and may bring attention to the colony. Is that true?"

"Have you known him to be the most honest individual?" Gia replied.

Anyway, Gia knew she had a nuclear bomb to set off on Kostas. She could always tell them that he'd broken rule number one and intentionally shown his tail in the world of Man. The only reason she hadn't already exposed him was that she wasn't sure exactly what else he knew.

Manipulating Kostas was easy, but her grandparents? No way.

They were almost two centuries old. They'd seen it all. She figured that if she kept quiet, Kostas would, too. It was an uneasy alliance, but the best option considering the circumstances.

At the other end of the table, Vittore and Stavros chatted away like old friends. Vittore's animated gestures were on full display as he told Stavros all that had transpired since they parted ways at Cold Currents so many years ago. Then it was time for Stavros to tell his tale.

"Try as they might, my sons and nephews were not able to pull me from the grip of the current. I slipped away from them. I tumbled down, I cannot even tell you how far. To me, it felt like I had fallen through to the center of the Earth. I wandered down there for so long. I survived by eating stray fish and other sea creatures, which felt like eating my own tail. But you do what you must to survive. It was dark down there. I saw great beasts and even battled some. I had no idea how to get home, no direction. I was lost. Every day I swam, just hoping to see some way out or some sign of civilization. One day the floor of the ocean began to shake with such violence, I felt the world might crack apart. The rocks moved beneath me, and from the ground, there was an outpouring of fire, an explosion. I swam away as fast as I could. I waited such a long time before returning, but when I did, I was so shocked at what I found."

Stavros caught his breath and downed his cup of cherry wine.

"Go on! Go on!" Vittore said, jittering in his seat.

But rather than continuing to speak, Vittore watched as Stavros's face curled up in concern. Into the room had walked a very tall and robust woman. Her grey hair was twisted into elaborate braids, and on top of her head sat a ring of crystals with a very large, black pearl in the center.

Stavros whispered something in Atargatis under his breath. The crowned woman approached the head of the table to speak with Xania and Triton. Everyone fell silent.

She spoke in a mere whisper, as faintly as hair fluttering in a light wind. Xania and Triton leaned in to listen to the words of their queen, and when they heard what she had to say, they dismissed their guests. Xania told Gia to show Cameron and Vittore to their bedrooms and to meet them in the Great Hall. Gia did as they asked.

The queen had taken a seat in an armchair, but Xania and Triton paced the room. When Gia entered, they hurled themselves at her and screamed, "Why did you not speak of what Kostas has done?"

Gia figured he'd ratted her out, so she just didn't answer.

"This is the worst possible thing that could happen, Gia," Xania yelled. "Do you know that now, on the shores above, Man is seeing Mermaid for the first time?"

"I do not understand what you mean."

"Kostas is on their televisions!" The veins in Triton's necks were pumping hot blood.

Oh, fuck. *La Nonna's* other client had released the tape. Gia suddenly regretted leaving the burner phone on the plane, not that she could get phone service in the colony.

"How does this concern me?"

"Kostas has spoken with the queen and the advisory board," Xania explained. "This has consequences that are far worse than you can imagine. You have both compromised not only our colony but mermaid colonies around the world."

"Other colonies?" Gia blinked her eyes in confusion. "What other colonies?"

"Xania," Triton interrupted, "speak no more. We must first allow the queen to address our colony." Gia's grandparents looked at her with shattered eyes, shoulders slumped.

50

DECEMBER 14TH

"**E**at something, darling," Bronwyn pleaded, fussing at her husband.

He sat with his arms crossed over his belly, watching the wall of TVs in his wife's home office. "Not hungry."

"That's a first," Harper muttered under her breath.

"Royce, dear, you have not eaten since yesterday, and you're becoming very grumpy." Bronwyn picked up the phone to dial the kitchen and have the cook whip up something, but before she could, Royce swiped the receiver from her and hung it up with a clang.

"I said I'm not hungry!"

What had taken Royce's appetite was the fact that the "Mermaid Tape," as the media had dubbed it, was spreading across the news channels like a global pandemic. And he hated nothing more than getting scooped. In fact, Royce spent his adult years strategizing how to avoid it. What was worse was that he got one-upped by Goldie Stern, who had dated Bronwyn ages ago when they were all young, before Royce put a ring on her.

On the screens, there were loops and loops and loops of Kostas and his brown tail flopping about in that baby pool. CNN had called in a panel of marine biologists to debate the phenomenon and explain how in the world such a species had not been identified, even as we trolled the ocean floor with cameras. FOX was calling it a left-wing conspiracy, meant to attract public attention away from the election results. Univision was practically throwing a party. They had sent a crew to report live from Disney in Orlando and managed to find the one Spanish-speaking Little Mermaid in the park cast, interviewing her for prime time about what it was like being (well, pretending to be) a mermaid.

And on OTN? Crickets.

Viewers were either turning the channel or calling into the network in huge volumes to demand to know why they were not covering this huge story.

And there was another, less frenzied thread—but significant nonetheless—and that was "Who is Gia Acquaviva?" MSNBC had decided to dive into that angle. Little was known about the man on the tape. However, producers at MSNBC were able to get a line on him. Their sources revealed that he ran a popular nightclub in London called Zeus, so of, course, they sent a reporter there. They weren't able to find out much more, but the trail was heating up.

Harper took the remote and turned off the screens one by one. "So, what's the plan exactly?"

Royce opened his mouth to speak but closed it with a sigh. Bronwyn tapped her nails on the side table over and over.

"Come on, you two!" Harper screeched. "Snap out of it! The story got away from us... big deal!"

"Big deal?" Royce balked. "Big deal! Do you know how low our numbers are right now? Jesus Christ, Harper. You should be on the air right now, but we've got that nimwit covering for you. It's basically the news story of the century, and what do we have? Huh?! Barren desert, that's what! Not a goddamn thing!"

Harper sighed and looked at Bronwyn. "Mom, what's happening with Goldie? I thought he was going to license you the footage?"

Bronwyn would have arched her brow, but the fresh Botox would not allow it. "My calls are going to voicemail."

"Fabulous," Harper deadpanned.

"I think there's only one thing we can do..." Royce said, words bitter in his mouth.

"What's that?" Harper asked.

"We gotta call Blonde Wig."

Harper angled her head. "Why would we call the White House?"

Royce exhaled with a sharp gurgle, "Because, Harper, I'm going to call in one of my *big* favors with him, and he's going to call Goldie, we are going to get the tape for free, and then we're going to have Blonde Wig say that the whole thing is a hoax and *fake news*."

"What will that accomplish?" Harper crossed her arms as she stood.

"For one, it's going to give us access to the tape. And second, I'm going to ask Blonde Wig to give us an exclusive interview and tell our viewing public that the simple truth is that he personally reviewed the Mermaid Tape with high-level Pentagon officials, and they have deemed that the footage is an absolute and incontrovertible fake."

"Can we all just pause for a moment, please?" Harper sat down on the coffee table across from her parents. "Do you believe what's on the tape?" When her parents didn't answer, she pushed. "Mom?"

"I have no idea, Harper. I don't believe anything anymore with the deep fakes."

"Dad?" Harper asked.

Royce shook his head, side to side as if bouncing a thought around his brain like a pinball. He blew a load of air into his cheeks. "Having seen untold numbers of hoaxes in my career... my God... remember how everyone was on and on about the Shroud of Turin? I really have a stomach for these things. It's not ringing false to me."

"So," Harper put her fingers in her mouth and bit down hard, "you think it's real."

"I feel crazy to say it, but, yes."

"Um... Mom... I really need you to weigh in here."

"Darling, I already told you I just don't know."

"Okay, but... if it *is* true, then..."

Her parents nodded silently in unison.

Harper continued, "Then Gia... I can't believe these words are coming out of my mouth... Gia is a mermaid? That's insane."

"It is," Bronwyn replied, looking hypnotized and horrified.

"Call your brother," Royce said.

"I've been trying for days and he's not answering."

"How is that possible?" Bronwyn squeezed her hands on her cheeks. "Do you

think he's somewhere hiding with Gia?"

"Mom, I have my guys looking for him. There's no sign of either of them anywhere."

51

Gia darted for the front door, but Xania stopped her halfway.

"By order of the queen you are not allowed to leave," her grandmother said, holding Gia's hand.

"How long will this continue?" Gia asked.

Cameron was becoming concerned about why Xania and Triton were acting strangely as well as why they hadn't left the house since the queen's departure the day before. Gia had told neither Cameron nor Vittore that the tape had been leaked to the press. She knew Cam would freak out, and she needed time to figure out what to do.

"Your grandfather will be back soon, and we will know more then."

Xania dragged a chair from the dining room and propped it next to the front door, embedding herself in it, and staring up at her granddaughter with narrowed eyes.

Gia turned on her heel and crossed the house to the guest room. Cam was inside, staring at some jellyfish out the window.

"Are you absolutely bored out of your mind, *amore*?"

He put his arms around her waist and bent her backward, dipping her, before bringing her in for a kiss.

"In a magical underground queendom where mermaids have made castles and conquered global warming? I would say being bored is impossible. I'm just restless. I want to get out there and see everything."

She rubbed the lines in his forehead with her thumb. "Do not worry, *dolcezza mia*, we will venture out soon. Shall we play a game?"

"Like a sexy game?" His eyes twinkled.

"I was speaking of a board game, but—

"I think that would be fun. What did you have in mind?"

"A bit of backgammon?"

"I don't know how, but if you teach me, I could. Warning you, though... I'm highly competitive."

She retrieved the board from the library and Xania shot Gia a dirty look as she passed by the front. The board was carved with mother of pearl and onyx, and it was very old. Some of the pieces were chipped, but overall, the set was beautiful. She and Cameron laughed and played many rounds until Triton came home.

Her grandparents came into the bedroom and interrupted a game where Cameron was in the lead. He was a quick learner, indeed.

"*Engoní*," Triton's voice was thunder as he spoke to Gia in Atargatis, "the queen has decided that you shall appear in front of the Council."

"The Queen's Council?" she inquired.

"The Pan-Atargatic Council."

She shrugged, trying her best to be polite, but still indicating that she didn't know what the hell he was talking about.

"Delegates from each of the global colonies will decide your fate, along with that of Kostas," he explained.

"A tribunal?"

"Of sorts."

"When is it happening?"

"In three days."

"I see," Gia bit her lip. Her mother had never mentioned anything like this. Mermaid court? It sounded absurd. Never mind the fact that, apart from myths and legends, Gia had always been under the impression that the only mermaids in the world were from her colony. In fact, as her mother had told her in many bedtime stories, Greece was the birthplace of the Mermaid.

How could they have kept these other colonies secret? How many were out there?

Gia tasted something acidic in her mouth. Her head drooped and her mind swirled. On land, she was a Shark, and she could maneuver her way out of any problem. Down here, under her grandparents' watch, she felt like a goldfish, small and trapped.

Would she ever be able to leave?

She felt the weight of millions of liters of seawater crashing down on her. And she had many questions to ask, like the rules of the Council and how she should prepare, but her mind was swimming, and she felt her heart pounding in her head. All she could do was lie down.

Her grandparents left the bedroom and closed the door. Cameron reached out for her, his eyes full of kindness. "What's wrong, baby? What did they say? What's happened?"

She couldn't speak, but just as she had done outside of Vittore's house on her birthday, she exploded with tears.

"Let me repeat myself again!" Bronwyn slammed her hand down on the marble countertop in front of Cameron's doorman. "I demand to see the security footage from December 1st until today."

"Apologies, ma'am, but we simply are not allowed to do that."

"I'm his mother, damn it!"

"Without a constable, I am afraid it is impossible."

"Constable? We'll do better than that!" She motioned to Royce to get his ass up from off the chair in the front of the lobby. "Darling, get the goddamn mayor on the phone."

And that he did. Within a half-hour, the mayor of London was at the desk between Royce and Bronwyn, and the doorman was singing a different tune.

A porter escorted Royce and Bronwyn to the back office and rolled through the film generated from various digital cameras. It took forever, but finally, on December 7th, there she was: Gia. Cameron's parents watched as their son rode down the elevator, met with Gia and an old man, rode up the elevator, and then came down again later that night with only Gia. On the footage, which was time-stamped as 8 December at 13:27, Gia and Cameron returned to his building and then left the lobby with the old man about twenty minutes later. None of them ever returned.

"She's got him," Bronwyn said, pointing at the monitor, hands shaking. "Call the mayor back. We need him to pull the CCTV footage from all over London. I want to know where they went."

"My darling," Royce said as he kissed Bronwyn on the head, "we will find him. Let's see if our guys can track down her plane."

"I've already tried that!" A tear was forming in the corner of her icy blue eye.

Royce cupped her cheek in his big hand, "And we will try again."

53

DECEMBER 18TH

The Kiwis were the first to arrive, a brother and sister—on the young side for mermaids—probably in their early 60s. Queen Zale, as host, had prepared her best rooms for everyone. Two delegates were set to come from each of the Pan-Atargatic nations. In alphabetical order, those nations were: Arctic Circle, Belize, Brazil, Japan, New Zealand, Senegal, and California. All in all, fourteen delegates from seven global member states.

Of all the nations, the only other queendoms were Senegal and California, though the Californian queen had declined the invitation and instead sent her two princes, who also happened to be the co-owners of a Silicon Valley Big Data firm. Every other Atargatic nation lived under democratic rule, so most of the delegates were presidents or prime ministers and their spouses.

Cameron and Vittore played backgammon in the Great Hall of Xania's house. Gia had not been allowed to leave the house in four days and was so impatient that she was ready to crawl out of her skin. Confinement at her grandparents' was even worse than being trapped at the Langley estate. Although Gia was half mermaid, she had spent nearly all of her life above the water, so she felt much more comfortable being able to see the sky. In recent reflection, she realized that the sky represented freedom, and she longed to be in her jet, free in the clouds, able to go anywhere in the world she wished.

Her grandparents had not given her any details about the tribunal and this made her anxious.

At least up top, in the cities where she maintained residences, there were firm rules for the accused. What were her supposed crimes? How much did they know? Was there no presumption of innocence under the sea?

Gia mulled over the options.

Was escape possible? Could she lie to the Council? Was there a way to shift all the blame to Kostas?

Cameron had been wonderful the past few days. He was patient, and she suspected that his calm presence had a lot to do with the fact that she'd broken down in front of him. She figured he liked being the hero, and so she remained mostly quiet. She explained to him what little she knew with respect to the trial, continuing to leave out the part about the now-infamous Mermaid Tape. He'd find out soon enough, and she hoped to deal with it when they got back on land.

In general, Cameron was still so taken with the magic of this place that he was a bit distracted and failed to absorb the reality of what was happening to Gia. In a way, he felt like he was on an extended ride at Disney—20,000 Leagues Under the Sea— having an adventure. And Vittore had also proven to be a great source of entertainment. He told Cameron many stories about himself, and Cameron indulged in stories about Gia growing up since she hated talking about the past. Luckily, there was enough to keep her man happy and occupied.

Gia had taken extra care that day to make herself look as glamorous and put-together as possible. She'd slept with wet hair tied up in curls the night before, so when she let her long brown tresses down, they were voluminous and wavy. She borrowed some jewels from her grandmother and applied a pinkish stain to her cheeks and lips.

With the late afternoon tide, Triton came for her.

"I will return soon," she said, kissing Cameron. Vittore pulled her down to him and kissed her on the cheek.

Vittore whispered in her ear, "I do not know if he has the same power down here, but I have been talking with our Father in the sky, and I have asked him to bless you and keep you safe. I have, today, a very good feeling, *tesoro mio*."

"Give 'em hell, baby!" Cameron shouted as Gia left, flanked by her grandparents. "Everything will be okay!"

Gia and her grandparents journeyed from Xania's through town via the main avenue. Everyone leered at her as they passed. Bad news travels faster than good, and the citizens of the colony, though miles away from any television set, were well aware of the Mermaid Tape by now.

The trio hooked a right and descended a set of stairs. To her great astonishment, what she saw below was a stunning vista. A very tall column had been carved from the rocks. She could peer all the way to the bottom of the cylinder, which was illuminated with more candles than she'd ever seen. They wound their way down the set of stairs as if traveling to the edge of a corkscrew. As they journeyed lower, the air became colder and saltier.

At the end of the steps were a pair of large driftwood doors.

"We must leave you here," said Xania.

"Whatever you do," Triton said, face stiff from trying to mask his despair, "tell the truth. There are grave and brutal consequences for lying." The last part made Gia's stomach drop.

"Go," Xania said. "Knock three times at the door."

Her grandparents left her alone and began the climb back up the stairs, headed home. Gia squared her shoulders and inhaled deep, yoga-type breaths.

I am innocent. I have nothing to hide. I am innocent. I have nothing to hide.

Then she rapped very lightly on the door, hoping no one would answer. But answer they did.

The doors creaked open. Inside was a small cathedral that had been carved from salt. A hint of sulphur lingered in the air, but it was overpowered by strong incense. Smoky plumes had been lit by each attending member state. Gia wiped her eyes, as the smells were intense: Palo Santo, Patchouli, Thiouraye, Plum Blossom, Ice Fir, Trikola, and Nag Champa. It was disorienting.

The Council sat in a circle. Her queen—Queen Zale—gestured to a salt bench positioned in the center of the circle. Gia sat, balanced on its edge. In a far corner, she could see Kostas. He sneered at her.

Queen Zale rose, and so did the delegates. She motioned for them to sit. Her voice was soft, like a butterfly wing, but the acoustics made it seem as though she were whispering right in your ear.

"In the beginning, the universe was enveloped in a shell of darkness. In this shell, Earth began to form like a pearl. Light pierced and Earth rolled out, the jewel of creation. Some in the world of Man say that life began with Adam and Eve and a garden. But we are the keeper of the sacred truth. We are the primordial creatures. Man is but a child. We know that all life was born of the ocean. All life depends upon the ocean, and all life returns to the ocean. O Gracious Tides, bless the Nations of Atargatis, we are few."

The circle repeated her prayer, "O Gracious Tides, bless the Nations of Atargatis, we are few."

"Come, child of the sea, spawn of clay. Approach."

The queen beckoned her near. Gia walked slowly, on the balls of her feet. And as she neared, the old woman reached out and clutched her chin. Zale's eyes were halos of bright gold around pupils so dark that Gia thought they might be twin black holes that led back to the beginning of time.

"Round the circle, child."

The prime minister of the colony in Belize called her over. One by one, the leaders looked her in the eyes.

When she made her way to the queen of Senegal, Gia felt comforted, because the woman's eyes arched up in a smile. The queen had a pink mohawk, and warm, caring brown eyes. After everyone had taken an uncomfortable gander into Gia's soul, she returned to the hot seat.

"The inquiry may begin," Queen Zale whispered.

A delegate from Japan began. "Have you caused harm to this man, Kostas Arethousa, as he claims?"

"Harmed him?" Gia replied. "I gave him a job, and I trusted him, and he stole from me. Pardon me, but if anyone has been harmed, it is only myself."

"He says you have killed," a woman's voice boomed from behind Gia. She turned to face the Senegalese queen. "Have you killed a man?" she continued.

In Gia's mind, her grandfather's warning echoed.

"Have you?" Gia retorted, trying to keep her voice from cracking.

"You are a bold one," said the queen of Senegal, "but I demand an answer. Are you a killer?"

"Yes."

A few gasps fell. One of the representatives of New Zealand shook his head.

"Was the killing in self-defense?" asked one of the two Californian tech moguls.

"No."

"Why then?" asked the other Californian.

Gia exhaled and bit her lip. "Have you all come here to put me on trial for murder? Or are you here because he—" she pointed a sharp finger at Kostas, "my own cousin, betrayed all of us to the world of Man?"

"Admittedly true," said the Japanese delegate. "Though he says he did so because you threatened him. He wanted to leave your service, but you would not allow him his freedom."

"Freedom! I told him many times that he was free to return to Greece."

"Wait," said one of the Californians, "did you not say that he was only allowed to work for you?"

"I do not recall saying that."

"A *falsehood*," Queen Zale's whisper splashed through the room like a tidal wave. "Child, you shall tell the truth to us or face the consequences."

Gia's heart beat unevenly.

"Come, Kostas," said the queen of Senegal. "Repeat your words."

"Gia is a monster. She robbed me of my chance to make it on my own. She moves all of us around as she wishes. We have no say in the matter. I have seen her on many occasions with men who later disappear or turn up murdered. While I do not have proof, I do believe she murdered a Spanish lover, and, with a little time, I could find evidence. She has made other members of the family lie for her and cover up her crimes."

The Japanese delegate furrowed his brow. "Is this true?"

"Which part?" Gia replied evenly.

"Tut-tut," said the Senegalese queen. "You are obfuscating. You have said you are a killer, so I believe you to be a killer. Have you killed one man? Or many, many men? No matter, it is the same. I do tend to agree with you, though. The focus of our inquiry is the revelation of the world of Mermaid to the world of Man. I have heard enough. I move to advance to sentencing."

"I second the motion," said the prime minister of Belize.

One of the tech bros raised his hand. "I move for ex-communication for both Gia Acquaviva and Kostas Arethousa."

"Harsh," said the queen of Senegal, "too harsh, I believe. I move for choice of punishment."

"Seconded," said one of the Brazilians.

Queen Zale rose and took one hand from Kostas and one from Gia. "Children, you may choose imprisonment, excommunication, or death."

Death? Death! Horrible choices all three.

The queen squeezed Kostas's hand. "Imprisonment," he said, face cast down, not meeting her eyes.

All Gia could think was that she wanted to get the fuck out of this crazy place as soon as possible, before the Council drowned her or fed her to sharks or whatever form "death" took here.

"Pardon me," Gia addressed the Council, "I am not familiar with these customs. What does excommunication mean?"

"For one thing," said one of the California guys, "you cannot come back here."

"That is correct," continued the other. "It also means you no longer have the support of the colony."

"What support?" Gia asked.

The brothers exchanged a glance and snickered at her obtuseness. "It means no more mermaid cousins running your businesses. Good luck with all that. You should be fine, Gia. Business empires practically run themselves, right?"

"*Bene, allora,* I choose excommunication," Gia mumbled.

"Mark the tally," said Queen Zale. "Ayes to my right, nays to my left."

Gia wanted to ask what would happen if they all voted "no," but that outcome seemed highly unlikely, so she kept her mouth shut.

The first to vote was the glorious queen of Senegal, who strode to the left, voting no. Her Queen Consort, another beautiful Black woman followed and took the queen's hands as they looked on with a vibe of silent support.

At least Gia had the lesbians on her side.

The princes from California voted yes, as did the delegates from Japan. The Brazilians joined the Senegalese glamazons in the "no" group. The representatives from Belize had a hard time deciding, but they ultimately voted yes. Watching the vote from a distance, Kostas scrunched his face up, inwardly cursing his cousin.

The representatives from the Arctic Circle joined Brazil and Senegal.

The vote was split. Three nations in favor of punishment, three nations against.

It was time for New Zealand to vote. One delegate took a step, then paused and went in the other direction, to vote yes. The final delegate looked back and forth at both sides. One of the Californian princes motioned with his head for the Kiwi to *get the hell over here*, but that seemed to annoy the delegate, so to spite him, she joined the "no" group.

And there they were, back at a split vote.

Hung jury? Were they free to go now?

Queen Zale, with her holy, golden eyes gazed at her wayward children, said, "Failure must be met with consequence."

She walked backward and joined the group voting yes to punishment.

Their fates were sealed. Kostas cried into his hands.

The Council members turned inward to their groups and began chatting—it was clear the meeting was over. The doors to the Salt Cathedral opened, and someone came and took Kostas away. A stranger approached Gia to escort her out. She walked over to the group who had voted in her favor.

"Thank you for your support," she said.

"I hear you must leave tonight," the queen of Senegal murmured, coming closer. She dropped her voice to a practically inaudible whisper. "Find my son in Dakar. My name is Awa. He is Moussa. Swim safe, child and beware of Man."

54

DECEMBER 18TH

"Be well, Gia," Xania said as she embraced her granddaughter, knowing it was likely the last time she would ever see her.

Triton held out the lantern and gazed out at nothing. "Do you need help preparing the boat?"

"Yes, Grandfather, thank you."

Great Uncle Stavros had joined them on the journey back to the beach. He squeezed Gia very tightly. "I care very little what that Council says," he held back tears as he spoke. "If you need me, then you call on me. If they want to excommunicate me also, then so be it."

"I love you, Uncle." She kissed him on the cheek. "I do need something."

"Name it."

"Please, can you take Vittore with you to Santorini? I will send for him as soon as I can. He is too old to take the journey that I must make now."

"Of course. I owe him for saving Marina's life all those years ago. I will settle that debt now with great pleasure." He embraced her again and then strutted over to Vittore and guffawed, "From one very old man to another, I have been ordered to take you with me to Santorini and get you very drunk for many days!"

Vittore's mouth hung sadly, and he studied Gia's face. "*Tesoro mio,* what is this?"

"*Methusalamme,*" her voice wavered, "I must go the next bit on my own with Cameron."

"You do not want me with you?"

"Do not worry!" Gia replied kindly. "Cameron and I will take care of one another."

"But Gia, what has happened? I do not understand. You have been so quiet and evasive these last several days."

She switched to English so Cam could understand. "There is something I have waited to tell you until we were on land." She scanned their faces. "The media has the tape of Kostas. That is why I must leave."

"Why?" Cameron's voice boomed. "The tape was his fault! You didn't have anything to do with it!"

"Unfortunately the Council does not agree. I have been excommunicated, you see."

"Oh, Gia, no." Vittore rested his head on her.

"Hold on," Cameron's face turned red with anger, "so that motherfucker from the other plane put the tape out there anyway, even after you paid him."

"He did indeed," she replied. "I knew it was a risk."

"Shit," Cameron's mind began processing all that meant. First, the secret was out on mermaids. Second, it must have been a frenzy out there, and third, if his parents believed the tape, which he'd never seen and really had very little to go on, would they believe it? If they did, then what did they think? He realized he hadn't spoken to them in weeks, and they were probably very concerned. "I've gotta call my parents as soon as we get to your plane."

"*Amore,* we cannot go to my plane."

"What are you talking about? Why?"

"Because everyone will be looking for it. There may be press there now."

"Then let's go to your uncle's in Santorini and call them."

"No, we must travel to Venice."

"What! If you're worried about being spotted near the plane, isn't Venice the absolute worst place to go?"

"I do not have a choice, Cameron. The Council will no longer allow my family to work for me. I have to speak to Yiannis to see if he will ignore the order and stay with me. I need him, *amore*. I cannot run the business without him. He manages everyone. I have to get to him very quickly and make a plan. We will need to replace everyone, and we must do this with the utmost haste, or my businesses will fall apart."

"That's what you're worried about right now? Work?"

"What else should I focus on?"

"How about your personal safety, Gia? What about the safety of our child? Do you think that the stress of being chased by cameras is going to be good for you? For the baby? We just went through all this weeks ago for God's sake. It's non-stop with you, Gia. Jesus Christ. God only knows what my parents think!"

"Your parents?" Gia replied, contempt clear in her voice.

"Fuck, Gia, I mean, they found out from some goddamn tape that you're a mermaid. A mermaid! Like a fucking nightmare version of a Disney movie! And they have no idea what that means for their grandchild. They probably have some monstrosity in mind, Bat Baby or some shit that pops up in tabloids at the grocery store. It's embarrassing!"

"Do not speak to her in this manner!" Vittore stepped in front of Gia and glared at Cameron. "How dare you!"

Cameron had never seen the old man lose his temper, and it caught him off guard. He stood with his mouth agape.

"Cameron is right, *Methusalamme*." She stroked Vittore's bald spot before turning back to face Cameron. "*Amore*, please," She made her eyes wide and wet like a deer, "I beg of you, let me return to Venice to speak with Yiannis. And then, if you like, we can all go to New York to your parents' house. I can run things from there for a while, and if I need to travel, you can come with me. Perhaps you can even make some suggestions on how to run the business."

She hoped she sounded endearing. Gia and Vittore stood before Cameron like two lonely beggars. How could he refuse them?

"Gia," he said, rolling his eyes to the sky, "I'm saying yes only because I love you. But I swear to God, you have twenty-four hours in Venice to get your shit together. I'll wait and call my parents after that. They'll figure out a way to come and get us."

55

U nder the cover of night, Gia and Cameron sailed to a nearby archipelago, where she chartered a helicopter to spirit them to a Turkish island. They changed helicopters and flew to the south of Bulgaria before they choppered inland through Serbia.

In Sarajevo, Gia purchased a short, dark red wig and paid someone to buy new clothes for her. There on a TV in a bar, Cameron caught a glimpse of the Mermaid Tape. The patrons pointed to the screen, jeering and blabbering on. He walked away quickly and got into the car Gia had rented.

They drove for a long while, arriving at an old, abandoned airport where they boarded the final helicopter, which took them to the coast of Slovenia. From there, they traveled via boat to a harbor near Venice and waited until nightfall, upon which Cameron changed into scuba gear.

Around two o'clock in the morning, they powered a small rowboat with an inboard motor into the Venetian lagoon and left the boat under a remote bridge. Gia dunked herself in the water and helped Cameron dive in with as little splash as possible, then, she led him through the watery paths to her house.

They passed the Hotel Bauman. Gia's graveyard was empty.

A thought of leaving Cameron there and escaping on her own flashed through her mind. She could disappear somewhere in the world and say *fuck it* to everything, maybe raise the baby, maybe not.

She glanced back at him and found him holding onto her tail, mostly out of fear. The water wasn't even that deep. But when her eyes shone on him, she remembered that she did love him, and, so she kept on propelling them toward home. She opened the secret hatch into her pool and they both swam in.

Once they came up for air in her courtyard, their motion triggered Harper's security cameras. Inside the wall, undetected, a light went on and began recording Gia and Cameron.

The motion, in turn, also set off a notification on Harper's phone.

Harper and her parents were in Spain, meeting with Nico's mother and gathering intel on Gia. They had not given up hope and did not believe that Gia had disposed of Cameron. Harper excitedly showed her mother the phone's display and they both cried with relief upon realizing that he was indeed alive.

Cameron was exhausted. Days of travel had worn him out, and he missed his own bed. Gia left him in her bedroom at the palazzo, and he took a very hot shower and changed clothes.

Being back at Gia's had him feeling unsettled––spooked even–– and there was a certain nagging doubt settling into his heart. Gia was in the kitchen quietly scrambling around making tea and looking for something to cook up. Cameron couldn't kill the urge to snoop. But for what?

He cracked the doors of the wardrobes in her bedroom and ran his hands behind her clothes. The smell of cedar flooded out, mixed with Gia's perfume. He opened drawers and closed them gingerly. He looked under the bed as though he were searching for the Boogie Man.

Everything was clear.

He shrugged it off. He was just tired and needed to sleep. Tomorrow, in the clear light of morning everything would be better, and he could finally reach out to his parents and they would be able to help get them to a safe place. He peered through a slat in the heavy wooden shutters of the house and saw several boats lined up, presumably photographers.

"*Amore*," Gia waltzed into the bedroom holding a candle, "I have some nibbles for you, a few things from the cabinet and the freezer, come with me."

She'd laid it all out in the living room on a souk tray on top of a big pouf. He was shivering, and she wrapped him in a wooly blanket.

"I wish we could light a fire, but we can't risk the smoke," he said. "I spotted reporters outside."

"I have an electric heater somewhere. Let me find it. Please eat." She pattered off, and he snapped a stale biscotti between his teeth.

On the hearth was the old nativity set, worn and sad-looking.

Gia had lit a few votive candles around it. He shuffled over and examined it. He loved miniatures. He reached into the barn to pull out a wooden horse, but he knocked over one of the wise men. The piece fell to the floor and shattered, scattering around the room.

Cameron crawled on his hands and knees to gather the poor broken man and make an effort to glue him back together.

The figurine's head had fallen into a grate inside the large fireplace. He stuck his finger into the grate to try to fish the piece out, but when he did, he scratched the edge of something else, something rounded and a bit cool. Bending his finger, Cameron succeeded in hooking it around the thing—whatever it was.

The thing he was holding onto felt something like a bowling ball.

How strange.

He moved the rusty andiron out of the way and lifted the grate, and found the wise man's head. It had fallen into the eye socket of a skull.

Swallowing a lump in his throat, Cameron plunged his hand into the ash. What came out was a bone, a large one. Other bones followed. He lurched away and rubbed his dirty hands off on his pants. He couldn't take his eyes off the skull. The wise man's head looked like an eyeball that had caved in. He stumbled slowly backward.

"Here we are," Gia scampered in with the space heater. "*Amore*, what is wrong?" Cameron's face was as grey as the ash on his pant leg. He was frozen in place, mouth slightly ajar. She looked around the room and then she saw what had caused this reaction in him.

"Oh, *amore*," she said breezily, rushing to him, "that is Mamma."

"Mamma?" He backed away from her, stunned. His teeth chattered, though he tried to stop them.

Gia inched toward him, and he slid back farther from her. "I... I had to move her. I wanted her to be near to me."

"Move her from *where*?" He cried, not really wanting to know the answer.

"Come to me, *amore*, I know you are very tired. We can go directly to bed."

"Why do you keep your mother's bones? Are there other... other bod—" Cameron's voice cracked, "bodies around here?"

"Of course not."

He kept shrinking away from her, but she was right on him like a shark that had spotted its next meal. They traveled like this, him walking backward and her lurching forward, from the living room into the foyer. Cameron steadied himself against the wall, feeling his way toward the door.

"I don't believe you, Gia. I don't believe you." The words dropped out of his mouth by accident. He'd actually meant to keep silent.

"Shhh, *amore*," Gia picked up her pace, so he did as well, fumbling in the dark. Inside her arms, her gills were aching, piercing her muscles.

"I love you, Gia. I'm sorry." Cameron turned the doorknob and bolted through her courtyard, running toward the exterior door that would empty him onto the canal.

EPILOGUE
CHRISTMAS EVE

I t began to drizzle, little pops of rain bouncing off the water. The reflection of a huge Christmas tree that lit the canal became blurry, dissolving into a mix of reds and greens and golds.

Cameron passed under a bridge.

The air was very, very chilly, but he couldn't feel a thing. He rounded a corner, leaving behind him a trail of blood.

A child bent over a bridge in the Rio di Cannaregio to toss a coin into the water and wish for an extra big present. The little boy held his hand out, but before tossing the coin away, he howled in horror.

His mother ran to grab him, thinking he was about to fall into the water, but as she reached the bridge's edge, she saw what her son had glimpsed, and she screamed as well.

Below them, Cameron's body wiggled in the current, throat slashed.

MORE FROM JINCEY

Love this book? Leave a review!

Dying to know what's next for Gia?
Pre-order the next book in the series today!